THE SORCERESS OF AVALON

A DRAGON-MYTH CYCLE PREQUEL

JOSEPH FINLEY

TARASTONE PRESS

ALSO BY JOSEPH FINLEY

PART ONE

BRITANNIA

CHAPTER I

THE BLACK SHIP

For hours, the black ship clung to the horizon like a hawk shadowing its prey.

Maugis gazed at their pursuer from the hull of the weathered, twenty-foot trading vessel they had procured in Mantes. The black ship was still a league behind, cutting through dark waters beneath a slate-gray sky.

"It's been following us since we left Francia," Roland said, his eyes narrowing as he watched the ship. The chevalier sat behind the mast on the forward oar bench, his jaw set.

Beside Roland and beneath the wind-filled sail, Turpin grimaced. His gray mustache bristled above a full beard that flowed to the top of his barrel chest. "At least this time it's a ship, and not a pair of demons."

That's an optimistic view, Maugis thought. The demons that had followed them to the Abbey of Saint-Julian-du-Fleuve six days ago were now imprisoned in a reliquary at the bottom of the sea, but Maugis still did not know who sent them. All he knew was that the man called himself the

"Blackbird." And right now, Maugis could not shake the feeling that he had something to do with the ship pursuing them.

"I wonder if your Blackbird's aboard," Bradamante said, as if sensing his thoughts. She sat beside Maugis, manning the steering oar. A strand of auburn hair blew across her forehead in the cold, salt-tinged breeze.

"I've been wondering that myself," Maugis admitted.

Turpin scratched at his beard, eyeing the ship on the horizon. "We know the Blackbird hired the two men who tried to kill you in Paris. And if he's the same one who summoned those demons, then we're in a heap more trouble than I'd like."

Roland glanced up. "I don't see any evil storms brewing in the sky, so maybe this sorcerer, whoever he is, is still in Paris."

"Let's hope so," Maugis said with a sigh. "Though if the Blackbird sent men to follow us, I've little doubt the abbot and his monks told them where we're headed."

"That abbot was an ungrateful bastard," Roland muttered. "After everything we did for him."

Turpin grunted. "You mean showing up at his gates with two demons in tow? Or maybe the horde of bats and rats one of them summoned while the other raised the bloody dead before burning half the abbey to ash?"

"We stopped them, didn't we?" Roland asked with a shrug. "A bit of gratitude *might* be in order."

"The abbot didn't owe us anything," Maugis said, "after all the trouble we brought his way."

Bradamante gave a faint nod before fixing her eyes on the pursuing vessel as it slipped between the white cliffs of Vectis and the green shores of Britannia. "If that is a ship full of men sent to hunt us, what do we do?"

"First," Maugis said, eyeing the black vessel, "we find out whether they're truly chasing us."

"And how do you propose we do that?"

Maugis scratched his close-cropped beard. "If I recall my bearings, this strait is called the Solent. It turns to river farther north, and about four leagues ahead lies a fishing village named Hamwick. If that ship's on honest business, it'll stop there. We'll row past Hamwick and keep to the river. If it follows us, we'll know we're its quarry."

"Then what?"

"Then we set a trap and ambush the bastards," Roland said, an edge in his voice.

"Right," Turpin agreed.

Maugis' lips curved in the hint of a smile. It was no surprise that Roland, Lord Commander of the Breton March, spoke of an ambush, but some might have been startled to hear the Archbishop of Reims so quick to agree. Turpin, however, was as much a warrior as he was a cleric, and a damn good one at that.

"You know we'll be outnumbered," Bradamante said, raising an eyebrow.

"Then it's a good thing, dear cousin, we have Maugis with us," Roland replied. "That Fae magic he's spent so many years practicing tends to even the odds."

"By God and good Saint Denis, it does," Turpin said, as all eyes turned to Maugis.

Maugis felt the weight of their gaze. He had asked them to take this journey, to risk their lives. They had all agreed, knowing the dangers, knowing what failure would cost. And he knew that without the Fae arts Orionde had taught him, they had no chance of surviving the mission.

With no time left for doubt, he turned to Roland. "We'll ambush them. Tell me your plan."

CHAPTER 2

THE AMBUSH

The black ship did not dock at Hamwick.

From the cold shadows of the woodlands above the narrowing river, Bradamante crouched and watched. The vessel was long and sleek, its hull dark-stained and weathered. A single mast rose above a gray sail stripped of any emblem, and no banner flew from its stern. But it was the ten rows of oar benches filled with men that made her draw in a sharp breath.

The ship glided upriver toward the narrow bank before two of the men splashed into the water to haul the vessel ashore, not far from where she and her companions had beached their much smaller craft. She counted the men as they drew chainmail coats from beneath their benches, along with padded leather vests, and pulled them over their tunics. Next, they donned iron helmets and hefted round wooden shields, along with an assortment of weapons: long spears with ash shafts, longswords, daggers, and throwing axes. There were twenty of them, all hard men, well-armed, and looking for a fight.

Four against twenty. Terrible odds. Yet she believed in

Roland's plan and trusted Maugis. And there was no real choice; the only alternative was to flee into the forest. And Bradamante was never one to run from a battle.

She stole away from the woods and hurried up the pathway that some huntsmen had cut through the forest. A half-mile from the river, she spotted her three companions at the edge of the woods. Like her, they had dressed in their armor.

"There are twenty of them, all armed," she reported.

Roland gave a half-smile. "We've faced worse."

Turpin cast Maugis and Bradamante a knowing glance. "That we have."

She answered with a slight nod, knowing they were right. But it did nothing to ease the tingling in her limbs.

Maugis pressed his hands together. "If we're ready, let's take our positions."

Bradamante strode thirty paces up the path before stepping into the woods and hiding behind the broad trunk of a moss-flecked oak. She removed her helmet and the cord that tied back her hair and let her long, auburn locks spill over her shoulders. She hated fighting without her helmet, but now was not the time to be mistaken for a man. Roland's plan required a distraction, and what better distraction might there be for twenty men-at-arms than a tall woman with long auburn hair?

As she waited, trying to steady her breathing, she glimpsed Maugis, twenty paces away in the woods, hidden from the road. He held his sword with a steady, practiced grip; the leaf-shaped blade caught the light as he shifted. Her eyes lingered on him for a moment before she shook it off, reminding herself of the task at hand. *Stick to the plan,* she told herself.

As the minutes dragged on like hours, she found herself tapping her fingertips against the pommel of her longsword. The wait was the worst part, but she jerked her head when she finally heard the chink of mail and the clomp of boots on the path. She peered through the gaps between the trees, catching a whiff of sweat and brine on the breeze. The men moved in a ragged column up the path. All were hard-eyed and brutish-looking. Some had weather-beaten complexions; others bore pockmarked skin. They all wore unkempt beards or thick stubble shadowing their jaws. Several had donned gray cloaks to cover their mail, but with their shields and weapons, no one would have mistaken them for anything but warriors.

She ran her hands down her slender mail coat and drew a deep breath. *Be brave,* she told herself before sliding her sword from its scabbard. She let its tip scrape against the ground as she sauntered onto the road, ten paces ahead of the column, her hair dancing in the breeze.

The warriors stopped in their tracks.

"Hello, boys," she called out. "What brings you here?"

"It's the woman," muttered one of the men, a blunt-faced fellow with a nose that looked as if it had been broken too many times.

"There's twenty of us and only one of her," she heard another say, a hulking warrior with a lecherous stare and gaps in his brown teeth. "This'll be fun."

"I want her when you're finished," insisted a short man next to the hulking warrior with a splotchy beard that gave him a weasel-like appearance.

"That's no way to talk to a lady!" Roland called out as he and Turpin emerged from the woods to stand several paces behind the men in the rear of the column.

Heads turned in his direction as wary murmurs of "Roland" percolated among their ranks.

Bradamante caught the scent of urine in the air; one of the men must have pissed himself when he recognized her cousin. These men were Franks, and she suspected many might have served in the King's army before becoming mercenaries. Everyone in the army had heard of Roland, and there was no chevalier more famous or more feared in all of Francia.

A tall man with a swarthy complexion spoke up two rows from the front ranks. "Lord Commander," he said in a confident tone that suggested he was their leader. "It's still three against twenty. Put down your weapons, and this will go easier for you."

"There's a fourth among us," Roland replied. "He's just not here yet."

"Three against twenty or four against twenty," said the leader. "It won't make no difference."

Roland grinned. "Oh, it will."

Bradamante cast a sidelong glance at the woods. A flickering blue light, like Saint Elmo's Fire before a storm, wreathed the treetops, and the knowledge of what would follow sparked a surge of confidence within her. Leaves rustled, the breeze grew stronger, and she sensed a sizzle in the air. Then, a howl roared from the woods as the trees bent, and a rush of wind exploded with the fury of a gale. But instead of sweeping outward, the blast narrowed before Bradamante's eyes, tightening into a spear-shaped cone that funneled leaves, twigs, and earth straight into the mercenaries' center ranks. The surge hit them like a violent wave. Shields tore free, and helmets ripped away. The blast swept men off their feet before slamming them into the ground, where a hail of debris battered them mercilessly.

The men in the front ranks who kept their feet were so stunned by the sudden attack that they did not see her coming. She punched her sword through the back of the first warrior. The man cried out in shock, causing the warrior next to him to spin toward her. She ripped her blade free and sent a backhanded strike that shored through the warrior's cheek, misting the air with blood.

Men screamed. In the far ranks, Roland's sword Durendal flashed, and a head flew into the air. Nearby, Turpin, whose bear-like frame towered over most of the warriors, battered men with his flanged mace as if they were whelps. From the woods, Maugis raised his leaf-shaped blade and charged down the swath cut by his windstorm.

In her left ear, she heard a roar. She leapt sideways as the edge of a longsword nearly grazed her shoulder. The hulking man gripped its hilt, the lecherous look in his eyes replaced by hot rage. "You whore!" he yelled as he swung his sword in a broad, sweeping strike. She tried to scramble back, but her heel hit something hard that sent her sprawling onto her back. The longsword scythed through the air, but the hulking man stared down at her, baring his jagged, stained teeth. She awkwardly raised her weapon as he drew back his sword, readying to bring it down in a vicious strike. The man roared, but his cry was cut short, ending in a gasp. His rage faded into a look of stunned confusion. He spun around, revealing a bloody wound torn through the back of his mail—and the man who made it: Maugis. He struck again, stabbing his sword into her attacker's stomach.

The big man slumped to his knees, clutching the wound in his gut. Maugis shoved him to the ground, then offered his hand to Bradamante.

A heat rose in her chest as she took it and let him pull her to her feet. "Thank you," she said.

Maugis' eyes locked on hers. "Of course."

She felt a strange urge to linger there, caught by his gaze, but with more effort than it should have taken, she pushed the feeling aside and fixed her attention back on the battle.

In the swath cut by Maugis' windstorm, a half-dozen men were scattered across the ground. Some barely moved, still stunned by the wind strike; others groaned from their wounds or lay lifeless, the earth around them stained with blood. Seven more lay either dead or dying around Roland and Turpin, which left three remaining. One was the group's leader, who, along with the other two, knelt on the ground, his hands raised.

Bradamante exhaled slowly as the rush of battle drained from her limbs. Roland's plan had worked. The fight was won, but this was not over.

Now, they needed answers.

"Have mercy, Lord Commander," the leader of the men begged. His face was ashen, and the confidence had drained from his voice. His chin, covered in a short, brown beard, trembled slightly.

Roland eyed the leader as he cleaned the blood off Durendal's blade using the cloak of one of the slain men. He thought the leader looked familiar.

"We fought alongside you at Eastphalia," the leader stammered. "Followed your orders, every one of them."

Roland narrowed his gaze, struggling to recall the man's name.

"Ludgar, Sir," the man said. "Don't you remember me?"

The name sparked a memory. "Ludgar of Metz? You were one of Ganelon's men, right?"

"Aye," Ludgar replied.

Turpin cleared his throat. "It's all fine and good that

you remember so fondly fighting alongside the Lord Commander here. What I don't understand is what possessed you to try to kill us."

Ludgar hung his head. "Lord Ganelon cast us out of his company halfway to Lombardy. Was a bit of a misunderstanding. But I—we, these men—needed money. We found a new employer in Paris, a generous one. He's the one who hired us. Paid us well. This was all business, not anything personal. I swear."

To Roland's left, Maugis let out a sigh. "Let me guess, your employer calls himself the Blackbird."

Ludgar's eyes widened.

"Who is he?" Maugis demanded.

"I don't know." Ludgar shook his head. "Never met him. He hired us through a woman."

"And what did she look like?" Bradamante asked sharply.

"Don't know," Ludgar said. "Hid her face behind a veil. But I think she worked in the palace."

Roland raised an eyebrow. When they embarked on this mission, Maugis had mentioned that Orionde suspected there was a spy in the King's court. Back then, Roland dismissed the notion. But maybe Orionde was on to something.

"What exactly did she tell you about us when you were hired?" Maugis pressed.

Ludgar chewed his lip. "Said you were headed to Britannia, looking for something. A relic of some type, hidden in a place called Glastonbury. The Blackbird wants it for himself, so he paid us to stop you from getting it. We figured with twenty men to your four, you might just surrender. No reason for this to get bloody."

It got bloody, alright, Roland thought. *Your blood, not ours.*

Still, the man knew far too much about their mission—

too much for comfort. Roland had only learned about Britannia and the relic when Maugis shared the secret with them a few days before they left Paris. It was a weapon, buried beneath Glastonbury Tor, hidden in a place called Avalon. A device to someday save the world, all part of some prophecy Orionde had shared with Maugis, if such things as prophecies were to be believed.

"Is that all you were told?" Maugis asked sternly.

Ludgar hesitated, then gave a nod.

Roland did not believe him. "Might as well tell us. This hasn't gone well for you, and it can get worse. I promise that."

Ludgar swallowed hard and blinked, unable to hold Roland's steady stare. "The Blackbird's coming," he said, his voice thin. "Don't know how long after we left Paris he followed us. But he'll bring more men, and he knows where you're going."

Roland's jaw tightened. *Just what we need,* he thought, *more bloody enemies.*

"So what do we do with them?" Bradamante asked.

Roland glanced at Maugis, then Turpin.

"Mercy *is* the way of the Lord," the archbishop said.

"Right." Roland leveled Durendal at Ludgar and his two frightened companions. "You will bury the dead and take anyone who's still breathing back to your ship. Then, you will wait for this Blackbird to arrive, and when he gets here, you'll tell him what happened today. And you'll tell him about the men you buried. And you'll warn him that if he goes after us, he'll end up like them."

Roland twisted Durendal and rammed its tip into the turf. "Six feet beneath the bloody ground."

CHAPTER 3

STONEHENGE

Maugis and his companions found shelter in a small priory dedicated to Saint Mary, nestled in a village called Downton. Unlike the pagan Saxons they had fought in Eastphalia, the Saxons of Britannia had embraced Christianity. They built abbeys and priories across the countryside, much like the Franks had in Francia, and this shared faith made them more welcoming to Christian travelers. Of course, having Turpin with them did not hurt. The archbishop was practiced in the art of dealing with abbots and priors, whose hospitality often hinged on the weight of a silver-filled purse. Maugis was always amused by how much holier men could become with the right donation.

The exhaustion he had felt after using the power during the battle helped him fall asleep, but he awoke in the dead of night, troubled by what they had learned from the mercenary leader. The thought that the Blackbird sought the weapon sent a chill down his spine. Did the Blackbird know about the prophecy? If so, Maugis had little doubt whose side the man was on. The demons that had pursued them to Saint Julian's were proof enough of that. Yet the notion that a servant of the Dragon might be racing to Britannia made his blood run cold.

By the time he woke up, a dull ache lingered in his head. He tried to ignore it as he and his companions ate a meager breakfast of hard cheese and stale bread, knowing they still had a long journey ahead.

They left the priory at sunrise and headed north, following a narrow, rutted path that wound alongside the edge of thick woodlands. The morning air was cold and damp. The trees were slick with the remnants of frost, and a gray fog clung to the ground.

Although it was not the most direct route to their destination, the path would take them past an ancient ring of standing stones the Saxons called Stonehenge. Turpin wished to see it, having taken a keen interest in stone circles ever since their ordeal in the Harz Mountains.

If I'm being honest, Maugis thought, *I'd like to see it, too.*

They traveled through a tapestry of gentle, rolling hills with pockets of dense groves of oak, ash, and yew. Around midday, the rolling hills flattened into a plain of windswept grass. An hour later, a faint cluster of dark shapes emerged, rising like a crude crown on the horizon. As Maugis and his companions drew nearer, the ring became clearer: an array of towering gray monoliths, twice the height of a man, weathered by centuries of wind and rain. They stood in a wide circle, speckled with patches of green moss, while a thin veil of mist clung to their bases like a ghostly moat. The surrounding air was still and quiet, and with each step toward the ring, Maugis felt a strange sensation as if he were approaching a gateway to the Otherworld.

Turpin scratched his beard, his gaze tracing the contours of the ancient monument. "I'd say those stones dwarf the ones we found in Eastphalia."

"I'd agree," Maugis replied.

The stone circles they had discovered in the Harz Mountains had eight or ten tall stones, but this one had more than twice that. In many places, pairs of these towering columns were capped with horizontal slabs, creating imposing gateways that led into an inner circle of smaller blue-gray stones. Most of the outer stones still stood, though some had fallen, sprawling across the plain like the remnants of a toppled fortress.

Bradamante's face darkened as she studied the circle. "Do you think this one served the same foul purpose as those we encountered before?"

Maugis' throat tightened as he recalled the unsettling rituals performed in those stone circles by the beings who built them. "I suspect so."

"What were they used for?" Roland asked. He was the only one of their group who had not ventured into the Harz Mountains on Hexennacht—*Witches' Night*—two years ago.

Before anyone could respond, a rough sound came from the far side of the circle. Maugis' hand flew to the hilt of his sword.

The sound repeated, *Ahem,* like a man clearing his throat.

Tearing Durendal from its scabbard, Roland spun toward the sound. "Whose there?" he demanded.

"I suppose I should ask the same of you," replied a voice from within the stone circle.

Maugis blinked. Whoever it was answered in Latin, even though Roland had spoken in the Frankish tongue.

Maugis searched for the speaker. He spotted him at the center of the ring, seated on a broad, flat stone. The stocky man wore the black habit of a Benedictine monk, his body hunched as he cradled a leather-bound book in one hand

and a goosequill pen in the other. His head tilted slightly as if sizing them up, and he caught Maugis' gaze with his one good eye, the other hidden beneath a dark leather patch. Deep creases carved his aged face, and his broad silver beard was sharp and angular, trimmed like the blade of a battleaxe. The hair surrounding his tonsure was just as silver, thinning into wispy edges that brushed the nape of his neck. Despite Maugis and his three armored companions standing at the edge of the circle, there was no trace of fear in his expression. Instead, his one eye gleamed with a strange, almost unsettling curiosity.

"Peace be with you, brother," Turpin said. From beneath the collar of his mail coat, he pulled out the palm-sized silver cross he wore around his neck and let it rest against his barrel chest. "We're travelers on our way to Glastonbury Abbey. We'd heard of this stone ring and wished to see it for ourselves."

"Oh," the monk said with a hint of excitement. "I know all about this circle. I've been writing about it for my book, you see." He blew on the open page as if trying to dry the ink before setting the book and his quill beside a small inkpot on the flat stone. He stood to greet them and strode toward Turpin. While the monk looked only a few years older than the archbishop, he stood no taller than Turpin's chest.

"My name," he said, "is Brother Meical, though some call me Half-blind Meical." He gestured toward his eye patch, an amused grin on his face. He extended a hand toward Turpin. His thick fingers were black with ink.

Turpin took the monk's hand and shook it. "My name is Turpin. I took my monastic vows back in Paris."

Brother Meical's grin faded. "I thought I was looking upon a mighty warrior. Did you abandon your holy vows for the military arts?"

"Alas, no," Turpin replied. "I merely ascended to a higher ecclesiastical office that permits me to wear this terribly uncomfortable armor and carry this heavy mace by my side."

The monk frowned as he glanced at Maugis, Roland, and Bradamante. "Are your companions also of your order?"

"No, brother, they are my bodyguards," Turpin said with a straight face. He could lie better than any cleric Maugis had ever met.

"They're accompanying me," Turpin continued, "on my pilgrimage to the abbey. I've heard the legends of how Joseph of Arimathea founded the holy site on the Isle of Glass after he fled Jerusalem with the Savior's chalice."

Brother Meical's good eye lit up. "Ah, yes, the story of Joseph of Arimathea and the Cup of Christ. The Holy Grail, as some would call it, brought by the great Saint Joseph across the desert lands and the stormy seas, all the way to Glastonbury Tor. Our abbey's history is quite magnificent!"

"Your abbey?" Maugis asked, raising an eyebrow. "Glastonbury is your monastery?"

"Indeed," Brother Meical replied with a nod. "And a very fine one, too."

Turpin eyed the surrounding stones. "You've written about this place. Can you tell us what you've learned?"

"Oh dear, yes," the monk said, a smile spreading between his bearded cheeks. "Let me tell you a tale."

CHAPTER 4

VITA MERLINI

A quiet settled over the ring of standing stones as Maugis waited for the monk to begin.

Brother Meical held out his palms as if to embrace the ancient stones. "My knowledge comes more from myth than history, but the tale of the great stones of Stonehenge is a story to stir the imagination. They say those stones were not of this land, but were first raised far away, on Mount Killaraus in Ireland. And not by men, mind you, but by giants!" The old monk held up his forefinger. "It was they who shaped the stones into a perfect ring, known to the folk of old as the Giant's Ring, or the Giant's Dance, depending on who's telling the tale."

At the mention of giants, Turpin and Maugis exchanged a glance. *Sometimes, there's truth in those old myths,* Maugis thought.

"Now," Brother Meical continued, "here's where the tale turns toward our own shores. In those days, the King of the Britons sought to build a great monument, a lasting tribute to the noble lords who had been slain in a bloody and bitter battle. But what stone could be worthy of such a sacrifice? It was Merlin the Prophet who spoke and said, 'Look to the Giant's Ring in Ireland, for no stones in all the world are like those.' And so the king, moved by Merlin's words, sent his son and the prophet himself, along with a company of men, to claim the stones and bring them to Britannia. And here, Merlin raised them once more, just as they had stood on that distant mount. Thus was Stonehenge born."

Staring at the stones, Maugis had his doubts. Giants may have created the ring, though it was likely built here, not in Ireland. But it was the name—*Merlin*—that intrigued him. Maugis had heard that name back at Rosefleur. It belonged to an old apprentice of Orionde and her sisters.

"In your studies," Maugis asked the monk, "what have you learned about this Merlin?"

"Oh, many, many things," Brother Meical replied with a broad grin. "He's the subject of the book I'm writing. I'm calling it *Vita Merlini, 'The Life of Merlin the Prophet.'* You've heard his name, no doubt, for the troubadours have sung of his deeds for hundreds of years. But few know the full tale of his beginnings. Merlin was born three hundred years ago to a priestess who held fast to the old ways of the Celts. His mother, they say, whispered to the spirits of the earth and sky, so from a young age, Merlin showed a hunger for the mysteries, the unseen truths that lie beyond the veil. He trained as a bard, learning the ancient songs and stories, but the songs were not enough for him. No, his heart longed for more, and so his feet carried him to the Isle of Avalon, the most mystical of places, hidden from mortal eyes by mists that obey no earthly wind. And there, in Avalon, he found his destiny."

Maugis' eyes widened. "You know of Avalon?"

"The old tales speak of it often," the monk said. "They

call it the isle that lies both near and far, hidden by mists that part only for the chosen. They say Glastonbury and Avalon are but two names for the same place, one rooted in the earth, the other adrift in the place the Celts called the Otherworld. It was there that Merlin encountered Nimue, the Lady of the Lake, and her sisters. The Faeries of the old myths, the ones who walked this land when the world was young.

"Nimue took notice of the young bard and drew him into her realm. In time, she made him her apprentice, teaching him the arts of the Fae: the secrets of the earth, the whispers of the winds, and the songs to bend fire and water to a person's will."

Maugis could hardly believe his ears. *How much did this old man know?*

The monk raised a hand and gestured west. "They say it was in Avalon that Merlin obtained the gift of the Sight, the power to see subtle signs that tell of the future. And so, he became Merlin the Prophet."

Brother Meical paused, letting the title hang in the air. "When Merlin returned from Avalon, he foretold the coming of a great king to save the land from its would-be conquerors. These were the Angles and the Saxons, back in the day when our kind were pagans, worshiping Woden and Thunor long before embracing the ways of the Savior. Merlin found that king in the nephew of Ambrosius Aurelianus, the last of the Roman kings, after the final Roman galley slipped away from our shores. His name was Arthur, the eldest son of Uther, the Pendragon. And thus began the greatest tale of them all. Though, alas, it must be a tale for another day."

Turpin creased his brow. "Why's that?"

The monk tipped his head to the sky where the sun was low, breaking through the clouds. "There's a convent dedicated to Saint Lazarus about five leagues west of here. We'll need to leave now if we want to get there before sunset."

"You're coming with us?" Maugis asked.

"My work here is finished," Brother Meical said with a satisfied nod. "I must return to my abbey tomorrow, and since you're going there, too, I thought you'd enjoy the company." The monk's eyes searched for something beyond the outer ring of stone. "Ah, there she is."

Maugis followed the monk's gaze and, through a thin veil of fog, noticed a gray, dappled pony chomping on the grass a dozen yards beyond the circle.

"Come now Lisbeth," the monk called to the pony. "We best get going."

The pony looked up obediently. A plain leather saddle rested on her back, with saddlebags slung over each flank.

As the monk gathered his writing tools and made his way toward the pony, Maugis leaned closer to Turpin and spoke in a low voice. "How does this man know so bloody much?"

"I was going to ask you the same question," Turpin said, equally quiet. "He does seem like the scholarly type."

"But he spoke about the Fae arts, with some fairly accurate details, too. How would a Christian scholar know so much about the power?"

Turpin raised an eyebrow. "You do."

"I was tutored by Orionde and her sisters. But there should only be one Fae left on this island, and I doubt this old man has met her."

Roland and Bradamante walked over to them. "Can we trust him?" Bradamante asked, casting a wary glance at the monk.

"He seems to know quite a bit about where we're heading," Roland said.

"That he does," Turpin muttered. "But maybe that's a good thing."

Maugis said nothing, though his thoughts were churning. As he glanced toward the monk, unease prickled at the back of his neck.

Who are you, old man?

CHAPTER 5
THE RUINS OF CAMELOT

"With Merlin's guidance, some say Arthur became the greatest of all kings."

Brother Meical brimmed with vigor as they set out for Glastonbury that morning. Still, Bradamante found herself wavering over whether to trust him. After all, it was odd—*too odd*—that this old man, who knew so much about where they were heading, just happened to be at Stonehenge when the four of them arrived. But he seemed harmless enough, and other than his pony, Lisbeth, he was alone and unarmed. And on the bright side of this cold and dreary morning, he *was* a good storyteller, and it was a seven-league journey to Glastonbury, so why not let the old man talk?

"Arthur was a mighty warrior," the old monk continued, "if the histories are to be trusted. They speak of his strength in battle and the fire in his heart, but even the greatest of warriors cannot conquer the tides of fate with brawn alone. No, to save the land from ruin and to drive back the pagans, Arthur needed more than mortal might. He needed a weapon, and that weapon was called Excalibur. There was no blade like it, nor will there ever be. Legends say it was forged in the mystical fires of Avalon. Some claim it was the Fae who created it, weaving their otherworldly magic into its steel. Yet others whisper that the sword is older than the Fae themselves, born before the world's first dawn. But that's the trouble with legends, they grow with time like moss on stone, and who's to say what's truth and what's fancy?

"What matters is this: Excalibur made Arthur more than a man. It made him a king. And with its power in his hand, he brought Merlin's vision to life. They say there were hundreds of kingdoms back then, some no larger than a small village or a single homestead. Most were petty and bickering. But as High King, with Merlin's aid and Excalibur at his side, Arthur united that host of kings and raised a mighty army to fight the pagans. Twelve great battles, they say, he fought. At Glein and Lennox, some far to the north in the land of the Picts, and then at Caledon and Land's End, and the City of Legions, in the place we now call Exeter. Two more were fought at Tryfrwyd and the Barrow Flats, but it was the twelfth battle at Mount Badon that the bards sing of most. For there, on that high ground, Arthur made his stand. Not as a mere warlord, but as the Pendragon, the shield of Britain, the hammer of Rome reborn."

Brother Meical raised an aleskin to his lips and took a hearty gulp before wiping the remains from his beard. "They say the pagans came in great numbers, their war cries rolling like thunder across the hills. For three days, the pagans laid siege to the hill, but Arthur's men stood firm behind their shields. And then, on the dawn of the third day, Arthur struck. He led the charge, his warriors thundering down the slopes like an avalanche of steel and fury, with Excalibur held high, blazing with the light of the sun.

"Arthur was a storm in the midst of battle, his sword flashing so bright it was said to blind those who stood against him. Wherever Excalibur fell, men died in scores, and Arthur cut through them as if death itself had come alive. Four hundred and seventy men, they say, were slain by his hand alone, and by the time the sun set, the pagans were broken. Their war leaders lay dead, and those who survived fled in terror, never again daring to march so boldly into Arthur's lands. After that day, Arthur brought peace to the broken land, ruling from his throne at Camelot with a band of noble warriors who gathered around a great round table. That was, until the fall, for as the mighty empire of the Romans proved long before, even the greatest of kingdoms can crumble and turn to dust."

The old monk gestured southeast toward a hillside. "The ruins of Camelot are over there. We may be able to see them soon."

As they continued along the road, Bradamante could not help but notice the similarities between this legendary Arthur and their own king, Charles. Arthur had a band of loyal warriors at his round table, while Charles had his twelve paladins. And just as Arthur forged a broken land into a great kingdom, Charles aimed to rebuild an empire that could echo the glory of Rome. She wondered what caused Arthur's kingdom to collapse and felt a tinge of unease at the thought that the empire Charles envisioned might someday meet the same fate.

"Ah," Brother Meical said at last, "there she is."

He pointed across a green valley that stretched for miles, ending in a broad, squat hill. Against the gray sky, the remains of what might have been a wall and a tower or two crowned its summit.

"They say Camelot was the jewel of Arthur's kingdom," the monk continued. "A beacon of light during a dark age, but also one of shadows, for no place can escape the flaws of those who hold it. Even within its mighty walls, betrayal and sorrow took root, and the dream began to shatter."

Roland's eyes narrowed as he peered at the faraway ruin. "Why did it fall?"

The old monk frowned. "It all comes back to Avalon, I fear, that most mystical and dangerous place."

Maugis stared at the monk. "Avalon?"

"Indeed," Brother Meical said. "You see, there was a time when Arthur fell under the spell of a damsel from the Lake, a Fae enchantress known by some as Morgain and by others as Morgana. Morgana the Fae, they called her, the sorceress of Avalon."

At the mention of Morgain's name, Bradamante's stomach lurched. She knew that name, and the memory still burned as sharp as a blade.

Brother Meical's gaze shifted to Maugis, whose jaw was tightening, and then back to Bradamante, curiosity glinting in his one good eye. But he offered no remark before resuming his tale.

"For a time, Morgain held his heart in secret, but when Arthur set his gaze upon Guinevere, the maiden destined to be his queen, he turned away from Morgain and forsook her. Yet Morgain was not one to be cast aside. Scorned and bitter, she set her craft to work and laid her snares in the shadows of Arthur's court. As her weapon, she chose Arthur's most trusted warrior, Lancelot. She knew Lancelot had feelings for the young queen, and Morgain stoked those temptations into burning desire. When Arthur learned of Lancelot and Guinevere's forbidden love, it was as though the land itself groaned with the breaking of their fellowship. Betrayed by those dearest to him, Arthur found his heart shattered, and his strength faltered. The bond between him and Lancelot was torn beyond mending. It was the unraveling of the kingdom, the end of Camelot."

A silence settled over them before Turpin asked, "Where was Merlin during all this?"

"Ah," Brother Meical said, "the answer to that question takes us back to Nimue, the Lady of the Lake. The legends hold that as the years passed, the relationship between apprentice and mistress grew closer, so close that Nimue took Merlin as a lover. And so Merlin's fate became bound to Avalon. Yet, much like Arthur, Merlin would, in time, give his heart to a mortal woman. Sebile, she was called. A beauty, yes, but human, and that, Nimue could not abide. Her fury was like a storm upon the water, and she struck Merlin down. She did not simply take his life. No, that would have been too kind. Instead, she wove a spell of binding, chaining his soul to Avalon itself so that he would never leave, never rest. And so, to this day, Merlin remains. Not dead, not living, but trapped within the mists. So, alas, he was not there when Arthur needed him the most."

The old monk's words hung in the air. No one spoke.

"Well," Brother Meical said, "enough grim tales for now. There's more to tell, but there will be time for that when we reach our destination. For now, you must excuse me, as I must answer nature's call."

As the old monk shuffled off toward a copse of birch trees, Turpin leaned in and asked quietly, "This Morgain he spoke of, is it the same?"

Maugis nodded. "From the grotto north of Verona."

Bradamante had little doubt it was the same woman. She hoped never to see her again, but she was not the problem now. "Morgain's not the one who should concern us."

"Nimue, then," Turpin muttered.

Maugis' expression hardened. "She's the last of the Fae

in Avalon, and Orionde's warnings about her could not be more dire. Nimue is the reason Orionde insisted I recruit each of you for this mission. And from what this monk has told us, folklore or not, our task may be more dangerous than I feared."

Bradamante exhaled. "It's not like we have a choice, is it?"

"No," Maugis said.

Roland shrugged. "How much more dangerous can this Fae woman be than the demons we fought in Francia?"

Maugis' jaw clenched. "We'll find out soon enough."

CHAPTER 6

GLASTONBURY TOR

They arrived at Glastonbury Tor an hour before sunset.

The Tor rose like an island in the center of a broad lake, its surface shrouded in a wispy blanket of silver fog that hovered inches above the water. A series of terraces, carved into the green-cloaked earth, one atop the other, ascended the hill toward its summit, where a wheel cross stood proudly against the dusky sky. A pathway zigzagged down the terraces toward the western base, leading to the island's shore. There, nestled at the water's edge, stood the abbey, a cluster of small, square buildings with thatched roofs surrounding a church with a narrow steeple. A ramshackle dock stretched into the lake, where a handful of fishing boats bobbed in the mist beside a ferry stand.

"Lisbeth," Brother Meical said, gently patting his pony's neck, "we are home."

Roland peered across the lake at the Tor. Somewhere beneath that hill lay Avalon, the home of the Fae woman, Nimue. She was the only thing standing between them and

30

their goal, and that thought unsettled him. After all, what was he supposed to do, kill her? Could a being like that even be killed? He wanted nothing to do with slaying this woman, and he did not like the idea of entering her domain. He preferred the world of men, where men could be killed. And Roland was good at killing.

But what good will I be in Avalon?

He wondered at times why they had even brought him on this mission. Sure, he had been useful against the mercenaries, and if this Blackbird appeared, Roland could kill him, too, along with whatever men he brought. Even at Saint Julian's, when the dead had risen, he had fought them well. Durendal cut dead flesh as well as living, even if the dead had a nasty way of persevering, no matter how many times you struck them down. But what awaited them in Avalon was unknown. And that's what bothered him the most.

Turpin looked up at the Tor, running his fingers through his thick silver beard. "What's that atop it?"

"Oh," the old monk replied, "it's a wheel cross, erected in honor of Saint Michael the Archangel. Someday, I'm told, they might build another monastery up there."

"How do we get across the lake?" Bradamante asked.

"Over there." Brother Meical pointed toward a cluster of tall reeds. Peeking through the gaps between the stalks was a wooden ferry, its weathered hull dark with age. As they approached, Roland saw that the ferry's sternpost was topped with an iron ring, through which a rope ran down into the water. The other end of the rope crossed the length of the ferry through another iron loop attached to the stempost and was secured to another post, half-buried in the earth and tangled in reeds.

Brother Meical guided Lisbeth onto the ferry, which rocked under the pony's weight. Bradamante followed, then Maugis, Turpin, and finally Roland. The old monk grasped the rope, preparing to pull the ferry across the lake toward the island.

"Want me to pull it?" Roland offered.

Brother Meical smiled. "That would be generous of you."

The monk stepped aside, allowing Roland to take the rope. Planting his feet firmly, he tightened his grip and began pulling them forward. The effort took more strength than he had expected, but he had plenty to spare. Gradually, the ferry moved into the lake, its shallow stern cutting through the silver fog as it drifted toward Glastonbury.

"You need to finish your tale about Merlin and the Lady of the Lake," Bradamante reminded the monk.

"Ah, yes, I suppose I must," he said. "Legends tell us that Nimue's jealousy did not fade with time, nor did her scorn, even after she cast her spell. No, her wrath was a slow-burning thing. So, they say, she has kept him there, in Avalon, neither dead nor truly living, like a marble ornament decorating a mausoleum. But the legends also say the spell is not unbreakable. Nimue's magic was not woven from love but from spite, though some whisper that love and spite are two sides of the same coin. And what lengths will one go to for love?"

The monk's gaze settled on Bradamante. "Nimue cursed Merlin because he gave his heart to another. And so, it is said that a kiss born of true love might yet break the spell that time itself has not undone."

Bradamante shook her head. "But Merlin's true love, Sebile, was mortal. She's been dead for centuries. There's no one left to wake him."

Brother Meical nodded, his expression unreadable. "True. Very true." He glanced toward the horizon as if watching something only he could see. Then, with a knowing smile, he added, "But what do the troubadours sing of? Love, once lost, may rise again, reflected in another's eyes."

Bradamante cocked her head and stared at the monk for a moment before looking away, her eyes narrowing in thought.

Hauling the ferry closer to the wharf, Roland frowned. He had no idea what the old monk was talking about. Why would they want to wake up some three-hundred-year-old wizard, assuming he was really there, wherever there really was? It sounded like madness. What they needed to do was retrieve the weapon. Get in, and get out. That was all that mattered.

When they reached the ferry stand, he helped secure the rope to a post, then moved to the side so Brother Meical could unload his pony.

"Come on, Lisbeth," the monk said. "I see a nice, warm stable in your future."

Turpin stepped forward and clasped the monk's hand. "We're grateful for your guidance, and fortunate to have heard your fine stories."

The old monk flashed a grin. "Ah, it was a pleasure, indeed." He gave a small bow. "Enjoy your stay at the abbey."

Turning, he began leading Lisbeth toward the stable. But then, he hesitated and glanced back over his shoulder. "And I do hope you find what you've come here for."

Roland watched the monk disappear into the stables, then turned to his companions. "He can't know what we're looking for, right?"

Turpin shook his head. "No, that's not possible."

"The Blackbird figured it out," Bradamante said.

"The Blackbird has a spy in Charles's court," Maugis replied, casting a last look at the stables. "This monk knows too much about Avalon for comfort, though he can't know why we're here. But we shouldn't talk about it in the open."

"Why not?" Roland asked with a shrug.

"Because our concern now is Nimue," Maugis said firmly. "And who knows if she has spies lurking in this abbey?"

WITH ANOTHER HELPING of Turpin's silver, they were able to procure the abbey's sole guesthouse. To Maugis' weary eyes, it was a cramped, one-room structure with wooden walls and a roof in desperate need of repair, judging from the wind that occasionally whistled through the thatch. Two rushlights burned from iron holders set into the walls. But it was the iron brazier filled with hot coals in the center of the room that Maugis appreciated the most, for it cast off enough heat to ward off the evening chill.

Once they each claimed one of the four straw-filled pallets that would serve as their beds, Maugis gathered his friends around the brazier to share a simple meal of day-old bread, pale yellow cheese, and a skein of ale Turpin had secured along with the room.

"Sleep while you can," Maugis said, sitting on the edge of his pallet. "Tonight is the last night of the full moon, and its light will make the gateway to Avalon easier to cross. We'll need to leave before it wanes." When his companions nodded their agreement, he went on. "Now, what I'm about to tell you is gravely important."

Bradamante exchanged a glance with Roland, then squared her shoulders. "Go on."

"Nimue, the Lady of the Lake, is dangerous," Maugis said. "Everything the old monk told us about her confirms that. My hope is that we can retrieve the weapon without laying eyes on her. But if we aren't that fortunate, Orionde has told me what to do. I'm to give her a message."

Roland let out a relieved sigh. "So we don't have to kill her?"

"I don't know if we could," Maugis said. "She's immortal, like the rest of the Fae, and she's been here since the world was young. Your sword, Durendal, is Fae-forged, so perhaps it could harm her. But I'd rather not test that theory."

"I presume," Turpin said, "Orionde believes this message will persuade the Lady?

"Not exactly."

Maugis reached inside his satchel and drew out a square of parchment, folded and sealed with crimson wax. The parchment caught the brazier's glow, its surface gleaming with a fiery hue.

"This letter contains a sigil drawn by Orionde herself," Maugis explained. "It's a symbol infused with tremendous power. If a mortal were to gaze upon it, the effect could be fatal. Yet for a Fae like Nimue, the sigil should be potent enough to render her unconscious, long enough for us to complete the mission."

Roland scratched the back of his neck. "And if this magic symbol doesn't work?"

Maugis' jaw tightened. The thought had gnawed at him ever since Orionde first placed the letter in his hands.

"Then we run like the wind," he said grimly, "and pray to God we get a second chance."

CHAPTER 7

THROUGH THE MISTS

Maugis and his three companions left the abbey's guesthouse before sunrise, armed for battle.

Roland and Bradamante wore helmets and mail hauberks, their round shields slung behind their backs. At Roland's side, Durendal's gold-plated pommel gleamed in the moonlight. Turpin donned his own helmet, his coat of mail draping over his broad shoulders and thick frame, his flanged mace dangling from a leather thong on his heavy belt. His shield with its iron rim and iron bosse was also slung across his back. Maugis wore no helm and bore no shield, but beneath his cloak, his mail hauberk jangled softly with each step. He gripped his quarterstaff, its hard ash wood blackened with soot and flaxseed oil, while his leaf-shaped sword rested in its scabbard at his hip. His leather satchel containing the book Orionde had given him hung from his right shoulder.

Their breath fogged in the bitter air as they made their way around the base of the Tor. Before they had set out for Britannia, Orionde had instructed Maugis to seek the white spring, a font of crystal-clear water that wells up from a hidden vein in the hill, spilling forth in a stream that winds its way toward the lake. He found it a half-mile from the abbey and signaled to his companions to stop.

Moonlight shimmered against a cloud of mist rising from the bubbling water like a ghostly veil. The mist concealed the mouth of a low cave-like opening, no more than three feet in height, carved into the side of the Tor.

"We're here," he announced.

Roland frowned. "This is a gateway to the Otherworld?"

"This is it," Maugis replied, sensing the subtle thrum in the air.

Turpin studied the spring. "The mist, is it a barrier, like the one in the forest at Brosse you told us about?"

"It shrouds the crossing between this world and the Otherworld," Maugis said.

"And the air." Bradamante stretched out her palms as if feeling something unseen. "There's a faint hum, like the buzzing of a bee."

Maugis nodded. "Yet another sign of a gateway."

Roland rubbed his chin, eying the entrance warily. "All we have to do is crawl through the water and into this cave?"

Maugis shook his head. "If you go in now, you'll end up somewhere, but it won't be Avalon. I've made that mistake before and found myself in a boneyard. I would have died there had Orionde not shown me the way out."

Roland's hand dropped from his chin. He stiffened, his gaze flicking between Maugis and the cave. "Right," he said, stepping back from the spring.

"It will take some light to get us there safely," Maugis explained. "I learned that secret years ago. Orionde spoke of it as a riddle." In a soft voice, he recited the verse:

Through silver mist where shadows sleep,
Bring light to crystal, bright and deep.
The veil shall break, the path be shown,
Where only those who seek may go.

"Soul light opens the gate," Turpin observed with a gleam in his eyes.

"All I need to do is summon it." Maugis curled his fingers into a fist, bringing the ring on his middle finger to his lips. Set into the band was a pale, square-shaped crystal. He cleared his mind, focusing his thoughts. Then he whispered a word born of the language of creation: *"Eoh."* Within the crystal, a spark burst into a radiant flash before settling into a pearlescent glow.

He lowered his hand and looked at his companions. None spoke. Bradamante's gaze lingered on the mist as if trying to peer beyond it; Roland's jaw clenched, his fingers tight around Durendal's pommel; Turpin crossed himself once, then let his hand fall away. They had all seen too much to admit fear aloud, yet Maugis felt it too, a quiet dread at the thought of what awaited them beyond the gateway.

He drew a deep breath and plunged his soul light into the mist. Then he turned to his friends. "Let's finish this."

BRADAMANTE WATCHED as the glow of Maugis' soul light parted the veil, carving a path through the mists. He crouched low, slipped into the cave's opening, and disappeared into the passageway beyond. She hesitated only a moment before following.

Dipping her knees into the cold spring waters, she crawled into the misty tunnel. A cold sensation washed over her skin, and buzzing filled her ears. The air felt heavy on her chest, and pressure built in her ears, but then, in a breath, the sound and the sensation were gone.

When she could stand up, she found herself with Maugis in a damp tunnel, where the spring bubbled up from the rocky floor. Patches of purplish lichen spotted the walls, emitting a dim phosphorescent glow. Beyond Maugis, the tunnel continued deeper into the Tor or wherever they now stood.

A moment later, Roland emerged through the gap within the mists, followed by Turpin. "Does it always feel like that?" Roland asked.

Maugis nodded. "You get used to it."

"Any idea what's down there?" Bradamante gestured toward the tunnel, feeling a lump slowly form in the pit of her stomach.

"Not really," Maugis admitted.

Turpin pulled his mace from his belt, gripping it in his right hand. "Then we'd best find out."

Maugis let the light fade from the crystal in his ring, then led the way down the tunnel. Bradamante followed, sliding her longsword from its scabbard and trying to ignore her growing unease.

The tunnel curved and opened into a broader chamber carved out of the rock and lit only by patches of the strange, glowing lichen. A warren of other passageways branched off from the chamber. Bradamante counted five of them. *Too many.*

"We're in a labyrinth," Turpin observed.

Bradamante's grip on her sword tightened. A fight in these tunnels would be chaos, and the thought of getting lost in this maze hardened the lump in her stomach.

"Did Orionde give you any clue how to get through this rat's nest of tunnels?" Roland asked.

Maugis' lips curved into the hint of a smile. "She did." He repeated her instructions:

> *When five paths you see, take the fourth from the right,*
> *Then choose the second where three split your sight.*
> *At the fork where the dark and the pale light meet,*
> *Step toward the glow, let it guide your feet.*

"Clever," Turpin remarked.

"We take the fourth from the right." Maugis was already heading in that direction.

Bradamante shrugged off a sudden chill and followed him. The tunnel curved again until it opened into a chamber with three more tunnels. Maugis led them down the center passageway, which twisted like a serpent before forking into two more passageways. The one on the right was thick with shadows, while a pale glow shimmered from the one on the left.

Maugis turned to his companions. "Be ready. From here, we enter Avalon."

Bradamante's muscles tensed. She drew in a slow breath, steadying herself. *I've fought monsters before*, she reminded herself.

They followed Maugis down the passage on the left, a short, straight tunnel that opened into an enormous cavern. Bradamante halted mid-step and sucked in a sharp breath.

The cavern was filled with a lake that glowed with pale white light, as if reflecting the glimmer of a full moon. In its center, rising like a mountain, stood an oak tree so vast she could scarcely fathom its size. Its thick branches twisted and stretched for hundreds of feet in every direction, and its top vanished into the cavern's dark gloom. Or was that the sky?

The tree had no leaves, as if it stood in the dead of winter, and its bark looked rough like ancient stone aglow in the lake's pale light. Yet built into its massive boughs, as if it had grown from the tree itself, were balconies and parapets, the remnants of a palace carved into the heart of the colossal oak.

"By God," Turpin muttered under his breath.

"The lake," Maugis warned, "is formed from the River Lethe. The name means *oblivion*. If you were to drink of its waters, you would forget who you ever were."

"Good to know," Roland murmured.

Maugis gripped his blackened staff with both hands and stepped into Avalon. Clutching the hilt of her sword, Bradamante followed him.

They were a third of the way to the lake's shore when she spotted movement, a pair of silhouettes standing in the water's glow. A chill slid through her veins. "There's someone here."

She narrowed her gaze. One stood taller than the other, their black robes swallowing the light. At their feet, three crouching shapes gleamed pale as bone, their hunched forms barely distinguishable from the lake's ghostly glow.

"Kneel," a man's voice boomed, "before the Lady of the Lake!"

Bradamante's heart lurched. *No!*

"Bend the knee," Maugis said under his breath. "We know what to do."

Bradmante gave him a nod. As she knelt on the hard ground, her muscles as tight as a harp's strings, she hoped Orionde's plan would work.

On the shore, the taller of the two figures lifted a pale hand and drew back her cowl. Though her face remained hidden in shadow, silver hair spilled over her shoulders, shimmering in the lake's moonlight glow.

"So," said Nimue, her voice cold and hard. "Orionde has at last sent her lackeys to rob me of what is mine. Who among you is her apprentice?"

Bradamante's nerves tingled with unfamiliar dread as Maugis rose to his feet.

"I am," he said. "But we are not here to steal, as you say. We seek only to safeguard the weapon and take it where it will be protected from the enemy."

Nimue let out a sharp, brittle laugh. "Protected? I have kept it safe here for nearly eight hundred years."

Bramante felt a thickness in her throat.

"Tell me your name," Nimue demanded.

"Maugis d'Aygremont."

"What shall I do with you, Maugis d'Aygremont—*Maugis the Thief*—now that you've come uninvited into my realm?"

"I would hope you let me speak," Maugis replied, his voice unwavering, "for I bring a message from Orionde, the Lady of Rosefleur."

Nimue laughed again. "What does Orionde the Traitor have to say?"

"My Lady warns that the Dragon's servants are growing bolder, and that it will not be long before they realize the weapon is in Avalon, if they have not deduced so already." He slid the satchel off his shoulder, pulled out the letter, and held it up. "My Lady suspected you would be hesitant to part with the weapon, so she is offering terms you might find agreeable."

"What terms?" Nimue snarled.

"I do not know," Maugis said. "My Lady insisted they are for your eyes only."

"Eadric," Nimue commanded. "Bring it to me."

The cowled man beside her started forward, allowing a clearer view of the creatures crouched at Nimue's feet. They were large, sinewy, and canine. Their coats, if they had fur at all, were short and pale, the color of bleached bone.

Bradamante gripped her sword's hilt so hard her knuckles turned white.

As the man strode forward, he drew back his cowl. He was barely more than a youth, twenty at most, and might have been handsome if his face were not so pale and gaunt. His robes were unmistakably Benedictine. But where a crucifix should have rested, an iron slave's collar circled his throat.

Eadric sneered as he reached for the letter. "I'll take that."

Maugis surrendered the folded piece of parchment.

Bradamante's pulse quickened with each of the man's steps as he returned to Nimue.

"Read it," Nimue ordered Eadric.

"No, my Lady," Maugis said hastily. "Orionde's instructions were clear. Those words are for you alone."

"*Read it!*" Nimue demanded.

Eadric broke the letter's seal and unfolded the parchment. As he began reading, his eyes widened, and then his hands began to shake. Red splotches formed on his pale flesh, only to quickly blacken, and smoke hissed from his skin. He let out a terrified wail.

"Deceiver!" Nimue cried. She thrust out her right hand, her fingers spread wide as eldritch blue light flared at their tips.

Maugis turned to his friends, opening his mouth to speak before a cry of sheer agony cut off his words. His head was thrown back, and his body arched in pain. His hands clawed at the air, and then he suddenly froze, as if he were a statue of a tortured man, while faint bluish flames licked at his skin.

Bradamante gasped as if an arrow had punched through her chest.

"Maugis!" Roland cried. He reached for his sword as if to charge the Fae woman, but Turpin held him back.

"We have to flee!" Turpin bellowed.

His words reminded Bradamante of Maugis' own. *We run like the wind and pray to God we get a second chance.* She cast a final glance at Maugis, then jumped to her feet and bolted for the tunnels.

From the lakeshore, a chorus of ghastly howls tore through the air, followed by Nimue's voice, screaming a command.

"Kill them, my pets, and bring me their corpses!"

CHAPTER 8

THE SORCERESS OF AVALON

M augis woke with a groan, pain pulsing through every inch of his body. He tried to wipe the sleep from his eyes, but his arms wouldn't move.

Am I paralyzed?

No, he could move his neck. He looked down and saw his armor was gone. Only a sweat-stained tunic covered his chest. Then he turned his head to the left and sucked in a shuddering breath. His wrist and hand were wrapped in glistening white threads, trapping him against a net of silk that stretched beneath his entire body.

What the ...?

Then he heard it: a faint, rhythmic clicking, like bone tapping against stone.

That's when he saw the spider.

It was larger than his palm, its sleek legs and body a glossy white. Eight black eyes stared at him, cold and unreadable. Its mandibles clicked again as it crawled over his wrist, spinning another slick tendril from its abdomen.

More clicking joined the chorus.

Maugis gave a sidelong glance. Three more of the hand-sized arachnids scurried across the strands. But to his growing horror, he began to realize this was not a mere net he had been ensnared in. *It was a web.*

The gigantic web stretched dozens of feet between the boughs of the enormous, stone-gray tree. More tree limbs spread endlessly above him, vanishing into the gloom. Maugis strained against his bonds, his heart pounding as he realized his ankles were just as tightly ensnared.

"Some believe the Lethe spider is the deadliest of its kind in all the Otherworld," said a woman's voice.

Maugis craned his neck until he saw her. Nimue stood on a stone terrace, as tall as Orionde. Silver hair cascaded over her shoulders, and she regarded him with gray eyes set into an ageless face. She bore the familiar beauty of the Fae, yet her cheeks were hollow, as if time had stripped away the softness. Gone were her black robes, replaced by a long dress of silvery gauze that clung to her hips and breasts, leaving little to the imagination.

She sighed. "What am I supposed to do about you, Maugis d'Aygremont? I suppose I could have my pets kill you. They would love to feast on your flesh. And it would be apt, after you took my Eadric from me with that nasty letter. He was such a pretty man for a monk. It will take me a very long time to replace him."

Maugis began breathing heavily as the cold sensation of being helpless coursed through his veins.

"Of course, *you* could replace him. Shall I make you my slave?" Her lips stretched into a wicked grin. "I might enjoy that."

She tapped her chin with a slender finger. "But not yet. Right now, you're going to talk. You're going to tell me everything that Orionde has been up to since the last of my sisters left Avalon for Rosefleur."

Maugis grimaced. "I won't tell you anything."

"Oh, but you will." She opened her other hand, revealing a small crystal vial filled with violet liquid. She pulled the stopper free and sauntered to the web. Her fingers, as cold and hard as stone, clamped around Maugis' chin. He tried to jerk away, but she held firm, prying his mouth open before pouring the liquid past his lips.

Maugis gagged as the liquid hit his tongue. It burned as it slid down his throat. He swallowed hard, choking on the heat. Soon, his head grew light, his body weightless, his thoughts unraveling.

He closed his eyes, but the darkness did not hold him. When he opened them again, he gazed upon Nimue.

She was radiant. Luminous. Like an angel.

"Now," she said, her voice as sweet as a song, "we will talk like intimate friends. Like lovers."

Maugis nodded. He felt an unyielding urge to speak.

"Tell me, Maugis," she asked, "when is the first time you heard the name Morgain?"

PART TWO
ANGELICA'S TALE

CHAPTER 9

MORGAIN

"Morgain ..." The name feels like a half-remembered dream.

When did I first hear it?

I search my memories for the answer. They swirl like mist, shifting shadows behind them.

Then ...

It was eight years ago. After Duke Hunald's rebellion ...

The mists begin to thin.

King Pepin had died the year before, his kingdom divided between his sons, Charles and Carloman. Charles inherited Aquitaine. That's where the trouble started, when Hunald sought to crown himself king ...

The mists begin to fade.

Hunald wanted revenge. Revenge against Charles and Carloman for what their father had done ... King Pepin had ordered the death of Hunald's father two years before ...

Now, at last, I remember.

Hunald and his nobles had formed a rebellion.

Carloman did not want to fight, did not want to go. But Charles did. He always loved a fight. By summer, he had gathered an army, ten thousand chevaliers and men-at-arms. We set off for Aquitaine.

To go to war.

I was twenty-two and had been Charles's vassal for two years. By then, he considered me one of his peers, one of his paladins. I rode in the army with our fellow paladins, and Angelica rode with me.

She and I were Orionde's apprentices, the only apprentices Orionde had ever taken in the three years I had known her. We were equals in age, intellect, and ambition, and ever since I returned to Rosefleur as the sole Count of Aygremont, we had been lovers, full of the thrill that young love brings. She was my first love, and we were inseparable.

Charles's nobles referred to her as "Lady Angelica," even though not a drop of noble blood flowed through her veins. Or so we believed.

Angelica had no memory of her parents. For as long as she could remember, she had been raised by the Fae of Rosefleur.

There, she had become more educated than any noblewoman in Francia. At court, her quick wit and sharp intellect served her well. But it was her beauty that captured the room. Her long raven hair, her bright green eyes, her delicate features. She carried an air of elegance, as much as any princess or any queen. My friends, Roland and Renaud, were infatuated with her.

But they knew she was mine. And I was hers.

The march on Aquitaine was my first military campaign since my cousins and I defeated my brother Vivian at Brosse, three years prior. But this one ended without bloodshed.

When the army reached Aquitaine, Hunald fled like a

hare before hounds. We chased him all the way to Gascony, where he sought refuge with his ally, Duke Lupus.

But power cares little for loyalty. By the time our army neared Gascony, Lupus turned on Hunald, delivering him to Charles along with Hunald's fifteen-year-old bride. The rebellion of Aquitaine ended with barely a blade being drawn.

Afterward, Charles remained in Bordeaux to oversee the construction of a new castle at Fronsac. That was when Angelica and I took our leave to return to Rosefleur.

As king, Charles could have forbidden me from serving two masters. But he knew who Orionde was—and, more importantly, *what* she was.

It also helped that a year earlier, I had presented him with her gift. The sword's name was Joyeuse, forged by the Fae from the same steel as Durendal, and it was one of the finest blades in all the world. With Joyeuse at his hip, Charles let me go, so long as I promised to return to him by Easter at Liège.

We had a deal, and I had Angelica, and life was good.

But it would not stay that way for long.

WE ARRIVED in the Val d'Anglin around sunset, a week before All Hallows Eve. Angelica and I rode together on Bayard, my massive bay stallion who, like Angelica, had been raised by the Fae of Rosefleur. She sat behind me, wrapping her slender arms around my waist.

When we neared the ancient forest that formed one of the barriers between the valley and Rosefleur, she leaned forward and whispered in my ear.

"No one will know if we don't show up at the tower until midmorning," she said. Her lips brushed my earlobe, sending a flush of heat down my neck. "I happen to know of a wonderful little cottage where we could stay the night."

Her voice was playful, and the warmth spreading down my neck pooled below my waist.

"Aren't you concerned that Orionde might discover our hiding place?" I asked.

Angelica scoffed. "Orionde keeps a mountain of secrets from us, and even more from me than you. So why shouldn't we have a secret of our own? The day she reveals all her secrets, I'll tell her of ours. But until then …" Her right hand slid down my abdomen, slipping below my belt. "Isn't the risk worth the reward?"

A rush of heat pulsed through my veins. "To the cottage then!"

I guided Bayard into the forest. The place was a remnant of some primordial time, where huge oaks stood bare, their pale, gnarled limbs reaching toward the dusky sky. A carpet of fallen leaves, crisped by early frosts, blanketed the ground and muffled Bayard's hoof steps. Moss-clad trunks rose over a labyrinth of brambles and thorny vines, more visible in the absence of summer leaves. Long shadows stretched between the trees, and it was no wonder that the locals believed the forest was haunted.

The cottage stood in the southern part of the forest, nestled a quarter mile or so within the woods. We had first discovered it in early spring, after the last snows melted, and it quickly became the perfect hide-away for two young lovers intent on exploration. Yet despite a dozen or so visits there, it remained a mystery why anyone would build a cottage in the middle of this inhospitable forest. Perhaps it had belonged to a woodsman, though no felled trees marked the land. Or a hunter, drawn by the abundant game in these unclaimed woods. Yet if so, why had he abandoned it?

Whether the builder was a woodsman or a hunter, there was no doubt that he had been a skilled craftsman. Its wattle-and-daub walls were as hard as honey-hued stone, and its woven thatched roof dipped and curved with charming irregularity. Moss and small wildflowers adorned the roof, adding splashes of green and subtle hints of color. Small shuttered windows peeked out from under the eaves, and a sturdy wooden door painted mint green welcomed anyone who approached.

Yet for all its warmth, something about the place defied explanation. The forest had not reclaimed it. No creeping ivy strangled its walls, no brambles clawed at its threshold. The underbrush that should have devoured its foundation had stopped short, as if reluctant to cross an unseen boundary. It was as if the cottage itself carried a subtle magic that kept the forest at bay.

Angelica tightened her grip around my waist as we approached. When we arrived, she slid gracefully off Bayard's back. After I dismounted, she threw her arms around my neck and guided me to her lips. Her lips were warm and soft. We kissed the way young lovers do, deeply, hungrily, as if the moment might last forever.

When she drew away, she tapped a finger to my chest. "This lady wishes the dashing Count of Aygremont to whisk her off to his bed chamber."

With an eager grin, I held out a hand as a lord might at a dance. "As you wish, my lady."

She took it, and I led her to the door. As expected, it was unlocked.

As I stepped inside, I expected the stale breath of dust and damp wood, but instead, the air was thick with lavender, rich and undisturbed. I reached for the small tinderbox in my belt pouch and lit a candle we had left on a side table near the door. In its glow, the honey-colored walls flickered to life, and a word escaped my lips.

"Amazing."

Everything in the cottage was just as we had left it. No signs of mice, no skittering beetles, no cobwebs clinging to the corners. The woolen rug covering the hard-packed earthen floor was pristine, as though time had never touched it. In the heart of the cottage stood a sturdy bed with a solid frame and a mattress filled with goose feathers, rather than the rough straw pallet one would expect in a hunter's abode. Above it, a bright wreath of dried herbs and flowers hung on the wall, still vibrant despite the passing months. The scent of rosemary, sage, and lavender lingered in the air.

Angelica began unfastening the brooch on my riding cloak. "Are you going to keep gawking, or are you going to take me to bed?" she asked with a grin.

I did not answer with words. We lost restraint quickly, and our passion swelled as our rhythm grew. In our excitement, we knocked the wreath from the wall. We didn't notice it until our pleasure had built and broken like a wave. Afterward, as Angelica clung to me, naked and breathless, she saw the wreath lying on the rug.

She lifted her head, eyes drawn to the wall where the wreath had once hung. Her mouth fell slightly open. I followed her gaze.

There, carved into the wall, was a name: "MORGAIN."

The name arched in a semi-circle above another, completing the curved shape's bottom half: "ACCOLON."

"Who do you think they were?" Angelica asked.

"I don't know. Maybe the huntsman and his wife who lived here before?"

Angelica sat up and narrowed her gaze. "Look, there's something more."

She traced her finger over a symbol carved between the two names: a circle divided into seven sections, each containing a letter. But these weren't Latin or Celtic; instead, they looked like symbols of power drawn from the language of creation.

"It's a sigil," Angelica realized.

Could she be right? My fingers brushed the gemstone set into my ring. I steadied my breathing, let my mind clear, and whispered the word of power into the gem. *"Eoh."*

A burst of pearlescent light flared from the stone, washing over the sigil. The symbols ignited, flaring with an eldritch blue glow, a telltale sign that the sigil was imbued with the power.

Angelica stared, wide-eyed, at the sigil's radiance, her lips slightly parted. The sigil's light cast a ghostly reflection across her face.

I swallowed hard and asked the question filling my mind.

"What is this place?"

CHAPTER 10

THE SIGIL

Angelica shifted against the pillows, tracing a fingertip idly over the sheets. "Maybe the woman —Morgain—was a witch?"

I studied the sigil and shook my head. "The craftsmanship is too refined. This isn't just a carving, it's a ward, perhaps designed to preserve this place. Whoever made it knew exactly what they were doing. I can't imagine some hedge witch understanding magic like this."

Angelica cocked her head, amusement flickering in her eyes. "Sometimes, I forget how new you are to all this. I've studied under the Sisters of Orionde my entire life. I think I know a thing or two about witches."

"The Sisters taught you about witches?" I asked, raising an eyebrow.

"They most certainly did," Angelica replied, a smug smile playing on her lips. "Witchcraft goes back thousands of years. Back to Babylon, and beyond that, to the days when the Watchers ruled the world. Witches back then understood power, the way we do now. But unless they were taught by the Fae, that knowledge faded over time. Today, most covens retain only fragments, much like the druids of old."

"I've heard fairy tales about witches my entire life. But if they aren't as adept in the power as you claim, how could a witch create a sigil like that?"

Angelica frowned, her gaze lingering on the glowing symbols. "Maybe Morgain's coven preserved this secret through the centuries. If so … what else might they have kept?"

I had my doubts, but we left it at that. We had planned to spend the night in the cottage and return to Rosefleur by mid-morning. Exhaustion pulled at me after the long day's ride and our vigorous lovemaking, so it wasn't long before I dozed off.

I don't know how long I slept, but I woke to darkness, the room still and silent, except for Angelica's voice. She murmured in restless tones, the words disjointed. I only caught fragments, something about a book. Then her breath hitched in a soft flutter, and she whispered a name.

"Morgain."

I reached for her shoulder. The moment my fingers brushed her skin, she gasped and bolted upright.

"You were talking in your sleep," I said.

She stared at me, her eyes wide. "Maugis, I saw her in my dreams."

"Morgain?"

Angelica nodded, exhaling shakily as she ran a hand through her hair.

"Are you sure?"

"She was tall, beautiful, but there was something wrong. She seemed distressed, as if she were in trouble. I swear she was calling to me for help."

She shuddered, her green eyes locking onto mine.

"Maugis," she said, her voice barely above a breath. "I don't think she's human. I think she's one of the Fae."

CHAPTER II

SO MANY SECRETS

The next afternoon, I went to Rosefleur's library to research magical sigils, hoping to find more clues about this mysterious Morgain and the symbols etched on the cottage's wall.

If you had seen Rosefleur's library back then, it was a breathtaking sight. It occupied four floors of the massive spire, each connected by a staircase that climbed through the center, resembling an array of enormous scallop shells spiraling their way between all four levels. Shelves upon shelves of dark-stained oak covered most of the circular chamber's walls, stretching upward to graze the twenty-foot ceilings. These shelves were crammed with leather-bound tomes and codices alongside stacks of scrolls, some encased in gilded or bronze cases. Each floor housed thousands of books gathered throughout the ages. In all of Christendom, I've never seen its equal.

Inside the library, the scent of old books filled the air, mixed with the sweet smell of parchment and the musky fragrance of leather. Faint sunlight spilled in through narrow, arched windows half as tall as the shelves, casting a golden light that danced across the patterns on the marble floors.

That day, I was on the library's top floor, seated on a wooden stool. This section of the library contained the most esoteric texts on mysticism, the occult, and the secrets men called magic. I was leafing through the crisp vellum pages of a copy of Hermes Trismegistus's Sixth Volume on *Hermetica* when I heard footsteps.

I glanced up to see Orionde and Una emerge from the spiral stairwell. Both wore the slender white silken gowns favored by the Fae of Rosefleur, though Orionde stood taller than Una, who was taller than I. Una's face, like Orionde's, was timeless and beautiful, yet with her coppery curls and sparkling eyes, she had a warm, inviting presence that made her one of my favorites among the Sisters.

Orionde, by contrast, carried herself like a queen, her long silver hair framing a face of serene authority. Although her appearance was breathtaking, she had a hard edge about her, the kind I'd seen in men like Charles. The airs of someone accustomed to command, whose authority was never questioned.

I set the book down and stood as they approached.

"Maugis," Orionde said. "Una told me I'd find you here. I thought you would have given me your report on Charles by now."

"I beg your pardon, my lady," I replied. "I've been distracted since my return this morning."

Orionde raised an eyebrow but didn't ask why. "From the scrying pool, I saw an army of thousands marching toward battle. Was there a conflict?"

"Not much of one." I told Orionde and Una about Duke Hunald's rebellion in Aquitaine and how Carloman refused to fight, forcing Charles to gather an army to quell the uprising. "I don't expect the Duke of Aquitaine to give us any more trouble," I finished. "Charles has secured the southern territories of his kingdom."

Orionde's face settled into a frown. "The brother, Carloman, is going to be a problem. A kingdom divided between brothers cannot be forged into the empire it must become. The sooner Charles deals with him, the better." She looked me in the eyes. "You must help him find a solution to that problem."

My jaw slackened. Was she asking me to help Charles remove his own brother and steal his kingdom from his two sons?

"When next you return here after a time with Charles," Orionde continued, "I hope to hear that he rules all of Francia. Now rest up from your travels. Your lessons will resume the morning after next."

I barely managed a nod before she turned and left.

"Don't let her words trouble you, Maugis," Una said, lingering in the chamber. "These situations have a way of working themselves out."

"How so?" I asked.

Una shrugged. "All men are mortal. Sometimes, they become sick and succumb to the fever, even at a young age. Others die in accidents, like the hunter who falls to the boar he was chasing. And sometimes, men die because of their ambitions. Some lords are not content to rule just half a realm, and their ambition drives them toward conflict, like the one between you and your brother, which brought you here. That situation worked itself out."

Because I killed my brother, I thought with a pang of guilt before reminding myself he would have killed me had I not acted when I did.

Una glanced down at the leather-bound tome resting on the stool. "Is there something you're looking for in the *Hermetica?*"

"Umm," I stammered, caught off guard by her question. "I came across some symbols during my travels. They looked … magical in nature, so I was hoping to find an explanation for them in this book."

A spark of intrigue flashed in her eyes. "Where did you see these symbols?"

"In an abandoned building outside Bordeaux," I lied, wishing she'd stop with these questions. "It may have been a tower once."

"How curious. Could you draw them for me? If I could see them, I might know which book holds the answer to your question."

I chewed my lip. "Let me think about them. When I'm sure I've drawn them accurately, I'll show them to you."

Una clasped her hands. "As you wish."

She turned to leave. Before she reached the stairs, a question formed on my lips. I hesitated, then asked, "Have you ever heard of a woman named Morgain?"

Una stopped. For a breath, she said nothing, her gaze sliding to the nearest window. "No." Then she went down the stairs.

But as I watched her leave, I could not shake the feeling that she was lying.

~

AFTER MY SESSION in the library, I found a note from Angelica on my writing desk in the scriptorium. She asked me to meet her in the garden.

Rosefleur's garden was not like a garden one might find outside a manor house. In fact, it was not outside at all, for nothing could grow in the barren, Otherworldly landscape that surrounds Rosefleur. Instead, it took up an entire floor within the massive spire, three levels below the library. The garden's arched windows were made of gypsum, and sigils etched into the stone walls used the power to control the environment. It was always warm and humid inside, and the air was laced with aromas of damp earth, fragrant herbs, and fresh green leaves. Grapevines grew on trellises along the walls, and throughout the chamber, huge boxes filled with soil gave rise to groves of fruit trees bearing bright red apples, yellow lemons, russet-colored pears, rich brown figs, and dark red cherries. More garden boxes were packed with mint, sage, and parsley, along with wispy carrot tops, fennel fronds, onion stalks, mushroom caps, and celery plumes. From huge baskets hanging from the thirty-foot ceiling spilled tangles of vines speckled with ripe tomatoes and peppers of various hues, green, yellow, and red.

At the center of this Fae-made paradise was a fountain that sprayed water around a glorious statue carved in the image of a leaping salmon. The fountain's splashing filled the chamber, giving the garden a serene, tranquil feel. The only thing missing was the singing of birds.

I found Angelica sitting on a stone bench near the fountain, snacking on an apple. She was wearing a close-fitting white dress, similar to those worn by the Sisters of Orionde.

"My Lady," I said with a bow, "how may I be of service?"

She patted the bench beside her. "Sit with me."

When I did, she gazed at me with a serious look in her eyes. "I need to go back to the cottage."

"So soon?" I asked, raising an eyebrow. "We can't be reckless about this. If we were ever to get caught—"

"It's not about being reckless," she said, cutting me off. "I can't forget last night's dream. Whoever she is, Morgain is in trouble. And I feel like she's trying to tell me something. If we go back, maybe I can discover what she wants of me."

"Do you think that's wise? We don't know anything about her. And if she can truly talk to you in your dreams, that's not some charlatan's trick. That would be a use of the power far beyond anything we've learned."

Angelica recoiled slightly. "Do you think they'll ever teach us everything we could learn? I'm tired of all the secrets kept around here. Aren't you?"

"I trust Orionde. If there are secrets she's keeping from us, there's a good reason for it."

"A good reason? Do you realize Orionde has never taken me to her precious scrying pool? Yet on the first day of your apprenticeship, she takes you down there and shows you God knows what. Something I was never meant to see, I suppose. But why keep it a secret from me? And this place—this Otherworld—it's a realm full of secrets. We've only been allowed to go as far as the border of the Riverlands, but what lies beyond there? They know, but they won't tell us. Yet don't you think we have a right to learn the truth?"

"They're Fae," I said carefully. "Maybe there are some questions that mortals like us aren't meant to know the answers to."

"Or maybe they're just afraid of what we might do once we learn the truth."

I sighed, realizing I wasn't going to win this debate. But something else weighed on my mind, something she deserved to know.

"I mentioned Morgain to Una."

Angelica's eyes snapped to mine. "And?"

"She claimed she had never heard the name." I hesitated. "But I don't think she was being honest."

Angelica's eyes widened, her fingers tightening around

the apple. "Don't you see? This is yet another one of their secrets. But this time, we have a chance to learn the truth, to find out why Morgain is calling to me."

I looked away. My better judgment told me there was something wrong about this, that we were delving into matters we did not understand. But Angelica persisted.

"If we leave after breakfast," she said, "we could be back before nightfall, and no one would be the wiser."

I sucked in a deep breath, unsure what to say. But then Angelica took my hands in hers, and her voice softened.

"Maugis, look at me."

I did.

"If you love me, you'll go with me to the cottage."

Slowly, I nodded. I could not tell her no. I was foolish back then, and I was in love.

But in hindsight, I should have listened to my instincts. I should have talked her out of going.

Had I done so, I may have spared us both the pain that followed.

CHAPTER 12
A FATEFUL DREAM

After breakfast, we set out from Rosefleur.

Angelica had thrown a white hooded cloak over her dress, while I wore my hereditary sable: a dark cloak, tunic, breeches, and boots with my sword in a dark leather sheath strapped to my belt. The tower cast a long shadow over the reddish landscape, smoothed by cold winds and cracked with narrow fissures that made the ground look like a mosaic of geometric plates. A quarter-mile away, the edge of the ancient forest formed a crescent around the area, and that's where we headed.

Not long after entering the forest, we encountered the wall of mist that formed the barrier between the mortal world and the Otherworld. I felt the dampness in the air and heard the subtle thrum that accompanied the swirling vapor. Before I could even raise my ring to my lips, Angelica had her own crystal, the size of a hazelnut, in the palm of her hand. She closed her eyes and whispered into the gem. *"Eoh."* Her soul light flared within the crystal, and when she aimed her light into the mists, the curtain parted as if bent to her will.

I followed her through the breach, glancing into the boneyard on each side, veiled in thick, gray fog. In a short time, the pathway cut by her soul light gave way to the towering oaks and crisp duff of the forest beyond the barrier. I stepped from the breach and set foot on Francia's firm soil. From there, we followed a winding trail through the woods until we reached the clearing where the cottage stood, looking the same as it had the day before.

"Thank you for coming," Angelica said, taking my hand and pulling me toward her.

"I have a problem saying 'no' to you," I replied before she kissed me.

"Why should that ever be a problem, Maugis d'Aygremont? Have I ever led you astray?" She flashed me a coy, beckoning grin as she opened the door and entered the cottage.

Following her inside, I reached out and pulled her into an embrace. This time, I kissed her. A strong, passionate kiss fueled by the desire welling in my veins.

When our lips parted, she looked up with a playful gleam in her eyes. "Now, tire me out so I can fall asleep."

Her wish was my command. We made love; afterwards, we lay spent together as the bed creaked softly beneath us. I had to fight the urge to drift off to sleep. I sat up in the bed beside Angelica. Her eyes were closed, and her chest rose and fell with each breath. As time went on, my eyelids became heavy, and I rested my head on the goose-feather pillow. At some point, I must have dozed off, for the next thing I remembered was a startled gasp.

My eyes snapped open. Next to me, Angelica's face appeared pale. Her eyebrows furrowed into a frown, and her eyelids flickered rapidly as if she were having a nightmare. My heartbeat sped up as I watched small whimpers escape her lips, forming into words.

"Book … shadows … Morgain, tell me …"

I wanted to wake her up and break whatever hold this dream had, but I reminded myself that this was what she wanted. It was the reason we were here.

Her lips trembled as more words tumbled out. *"Between the mother and the warrior …"*

She gasped again. *"Orionde … betrayer!"*

She reached out and grabbed my wrist; her fingers pressed hard into my flesh as she tightened her grip. I had no choice. With my free arm, I gave her shoulder a shake.

Angelica's eyes flew open. Gasping for air, she fixed her gaze on mine, and I saw tears start to well up in her eyes.

"Did you see her?" I asked.

Angelica nodded as she let go of my wrist. "Morgain's in trouble. She's trapped somewhere, a wasteland with black cliffs and a sky without stars. She told me Orionde betrayed her."

I shook my head in disbelief. "How?"

She looked away. "I don't know. Maybe she's the one who imprisoned Morgain in that awful place. But I know how to save her."

She faced me again. Her green eyes burned with determination, and her gaze sent a chill through my veins.

"Maugis," she insisted. "Promise you'll help me do it."

CHAPTER 13

A DISTURBING TRUTH

The cottage lay in darkness, save for the faint slivers of sunlight that peeked through the slats of the shuttered windows. Sitting on the edge of the bed beside Angelica, I felt a strange numbness settle over me. I could not believe Orionde would betray anyone.

But I had never seen Angelica look so vulnerable. Her hands were clenched in her lap, her breath uneven.

"What exactly did she tell you?" I asked.

"She said there's a book in the library that contains the words to set her free."

A chill curled down my spine. "What book?"

Angelica squeezed her eyes shut. After a moment, she let out a quiet breath, shaking her head. "I don't know if she ever said the name. But she told me how to find it. She said it's kept hidden beyond the dark side of the moon, which lies between the mother and the warrior."

"That's a bit cryptic. Did she happen to mention what floor it's on, or who these people even are? There are no statues, no tapestries, no images of people anywhere in the library."

Angelica combed her fingers through her raven hair. "She said she had no more time to explain. The longer she spoke to me, the more her image faded. I'm certain she's one of the Fae, but the power it must have taken to reach me from wherever she's trapped. It was more than she could bear for long. But she told me enough. We can figure out the rest."

I let out a sigh. "Why do you want to help her?"

Angelica looked at me, her eyes wide. "I …" she hesitated, pressing a hand to her chest. "It's more than just a feeling. It's like a tether pulling me toward her. Maybe she was at Rosefleur when I was young, and I've forgotten. But I feel her suffering, and I can't ignore it."

I didn't know what to say. I doubted Orionde would banish anyone to some hellish prison, and I felt wary about Angelica heading down a path she wasn't meant to walk. But I could see it in her face. She was troubled, and her desire to help Morgain seemed real.

She placed her hand on my cheek and asked me again. My better judgment gave way.

I could not refuse her, for I was in love.

And I was a fool.

ANGELICA and I planned to meet in the library an hour after sunset, when it would be unoccupied. But shortly after returning from the cabin, I went there, looking for Una and hoping to find some answers.

After my discussion with Una the day before about the symbols I discovered in the cottage, I followed her suggestion and drew a copy of the sigil from memory: a circular shape divided into seven parts, with a symbol in each one.

I found Una on the library's top floor. She glanced up when I entered. Through the tall, narrow windows, sunlight glinted off her coppery hair. "Here for more talk of strange symbols?"

"I sketched them out, like you suggested." I handed her the drawing.

As she studied it, her brow furrowed, and her gaze narrowed. "Where, again, did you see these?"

I repeated my lie from yesterday. "In a ruin outside Bordeaux."

"Hmm," she murmured. "Whoever crafted these knew what they were doing." She turned toward one of the towering bookshelves packed with leather tomes. "Let me show you."

She gently traced a forefinger along the spines of a row of books until she found the one she wanted and pulled it off the shelf. It was a thin codex with a leather cover stained so dark it nearly looked black.

"I've not read that one," I admitted.

She opened the cover and began sifting through the vellum pages. "It's a copy of the *Mysteria Symbola* by

Aqueron Lysander. He was a philosopher and a counselor to Arcanus, one of the Atlantean kings. The original was lost during the fall of Atlantis, but we persevered several copies, all scrolls, of course, when our kind fled to Éire. After we moved to Avalon, we copied this one as a book. They're so much easier to read."

"I can't argue with you there." I hated scrolls.

When she stopped flipping through the pages, she bent down and showed me. Two of the sigil's strange symbols were etched prominently on the vellum. "Together, these two symbols form the phrase '*Eol Vohim.*' It's a powerful preservation ward. It prevents natural matter from decaying."

I nodded my head. No wonder the cottage had withstood the ravages of time.

She skimmed through several more pages until landing on one that showed two more of the symbols. "These symbols are pronounced '*Uni Nalvage.*' It's another kind of ward. It protects against pests, for lack of a better word. The glyph is wonderful for keeping away spiders, hornets, mice, that kind of thing."

I gave another nod. "How about the other three?"

Una pressed her lips together before she spoke. "Those three are more troubling." She thumbed through several more pages before stopping at one depicting the remaining three symbols in the shape of a triangle. "The glyph is pronounced '*Bahal Aol.*' It means 'to cry out to the maker.' When exposed to the power, it sends a warning to the glyph's creator."

A pang of unease shot through my stomach. "I used my soul light to examine the sigil."

Una shut the book, a look of concern on her face. "Then let's hope whoever created it is long dead. The fact that no one came after you when you triggered the warning suggests as much."

I let out what sounded like a grateful sigh, but inside, I felt sick to my stomach. Using my soul light on the sigil must have triggered the warning that alerted Morgain.

Unwittingly, I had set this wheel in motion, and now I had no one but myself to blame.

CHAPTER 14

SYMBOLS AND WARDS

The library was quiet as a tomb when Angelica and I went there an hour after sunset. Although moonlight spilled through the narrow windows, I brought a handheld lantern the Fae had crafted after some Byzantine design for added light. It had a curved bronze handle and a bronze base fitted with small panes of wavy, hand-blown glass, enough to guard the flame from any draft and, more importantly, to keep the books safe from it. As we glanced around, the lantern's glow banished the shadows between the shelves and danced off the scrolls and leather-bound tomes.

"You're right," Angelica said, surveying the circular chamber. "There are no images of people anywhere."

I shook my head. "The only symbols are those marking the rows of shelves by topic." I pointed to one, which looked like a stylized lowercase "n" with a looped tail.

Angelica walked up to it. The symbol was carved into a foot-tall stone plaque set into the wall, slightly above her head, next to the shelves of history books. She traced a finger over it. "I know we've always thought of this as marking the history section, but the symbol's astrological, right?"

I scratched my head, staring at the plaque. "That's right. It's the symbol for Capricorn."

"Do you know the meaning of Capricorn?" she asked, putting her hands on her slender hips.

"I'm not much of an expert in astrology."

"I'm no astrologer either," she said. "But fortunately for us, we're in a very large library."

She took my free hand. "Come on." She led me toward the spiral staircase in the center of the chamber. I knew where we were going, for the astrology shelves were on the next floor up.

When we arrived, I noticed the stone plaque on the wall beside the shelves of astrological tomes. It depicted a pair of wavy lines, one above the other, the symbol for Aquarius.

"Let me have the lantern," she said.

I gave it to her, and she used its glow to illuminate the spines of the leather-bound books. After searching for several minutes, she pulled one from the bookshelf. "Let's give this a try," she said, handing me the lantern.

Looking over her shoulder, I held the lantern up so that its light washed over the book. I drew in a breath and caught the scent of rosewater in her long, raven hair. My free hand fell to her waist, above her right hip.

She opened the cover and read the title page aloud. "*The Celestial Tapestry: A Treatise on Astrological Symbols* by Claudius Ptolemy." As Angelica paged through the book, I noticed that each chapter focused on a different Zodiac symbol. She flipped back to the first chapter, which happened to concern the symbol for Capricorn.

Angelica wrinkled her nose. "The mystical sea goat, a creature with the front half of a goat and the back half of a fish, embodying the dual nature of the material and emotional realms. That won't do."

She turned to the next chapter, which bore the title "Aquarius" above a symbol of the same parallel wavy lines marked on the wall. "The running waters," she read aloud, "symbolize wisdom, knowledge, and the flow of energy through the world." Angelica let out a frustrated sigh.

"I have an idea," I said. "Go to the chapter on Ares."

She gave me a skeptical look. "The ram?"

"Humor me."

She found it, only two chapters away from the one on Aquarius. Below the title was a symbol shaped like the letter "V" and topped with two curved horns. "The mighty ram," she read, "named after the Greek god of war." She looked up from the page, her eyes wide. "A warrior!"

"I thought that might be the case," I said, feeling a surge of pride at having figured out the answer.

"That's only one floor above," she said, then let out a quiet laugh. "It marks the books on Warcraft."

Taking Ptolemy's tome with her, she headed for the stairs. I caught up with her and led the way, using my lantern to light the steps. When we reached the third level, we moved toward the shelves holding books on warfare and military strategy, the histories of famous battles, and manuals on archery and swordsmanship. As expected, a stone plaque bearing the symbol for Ares was embedded in the wall beside the first bookshelf.

"What other symbols are on this floor?" she asked.

I thought for a moment. "Cancer marks the shelves for books on cooking and baking, the making of wine, and the brewing of ale. Then there's the shelves on anatomy and medicine, healing, elixirs, that sort of thing—"

"Marked by Virgo," Angelica said before I could finish my thought. She opened the book. "Give me some light."

I held up the lantern as she leafed through the tome until she found the chapter on Virgo. "It says Virgo symbolizes the virgin." She groaned but kept reading. "In some cultures, she is the goddess, a symbol of fertility, springtime, and the natural world."

I sucked in a breath. "Mother Earth."

"By God, you're right!"

"So what's between the Mother and the Warrior?"

"Cancer," she said with a hint of excitement.

We set off along the chamber's periphery. After passing a series of shelves along the curved wall, we came to another plaque bearing the symbol for Cancer. Angelica was already flipping through the pages of Ptolemy's book. When she found the right page, she began reading: "Cancer, the great crab. Its claws' circular motion hints at life's cyclical nature, resonating with Cancer's ruling celestial body—the moon!"

I repeated the words Morgain had told Angelica. "The book's kept secret beyond the dark side of the moon, which lies between the mother and the warrior."

Angelica's eyes were aglow. "The dark side of the moon," she said eagerly. "The moon's other side, the part we can't see. Which means—"

"This must be a door!"

With my free hand, I pressed on the stone plaque, but it did not move. I studied the seam between the plaque and the wall, but it was too narrow to wedge my fingers in and pry it open.

"Maybe there's some type of ward on the door?" Angelica said. "Let's find out."

She drew her crystal from a pocket in her dress, but I grabbed her wrist before she could bring it to her lips. "Stop," I whispered. "Using the power could trigger the ward."

She glared at me with a mix of annoyance and confusion. "What?"

"Trust me," I said. "I've been studying mystic symbols, and there are glyphs that will warn whoever created them if they're touched by your soul light. So, unless we want Orionde to know we've been searching for this secret book, we need to find another way."

Angelica's eyes widened, and she gave me a slow nod. I let go of her wrist, and she tucked the crystal back into her pocket. "What do we do now?"

"On the next floor up, there's a book that might help."

She followed me up the stairs to the top floor, where I headed for the collection of books on mysticism and magic. I found the copy of Aqueron Lysander's *Mysteria Symbola* where Una had reshelved it earlier in the day.

"You've read that one?" Angelica asked.

I nodded.

"What is it?"

"A book on mystic symbols written by a prominent Atlantean philosopher."

"It's *that* old?"

"It's pretty damn old."

I handed Angelica my lantern and began searching the pages. After leafing through a lengthy discussion on various glyphs and symbols, I found what I was looking for. I read the chapter heading aloud: "*On the careful detection of seals and wards.*"

Angelica watched me with a look of anxious anticipation as I skimmed through the chapter. I glanced up as soon as I found the answer. "It's moonlight. According to the author, the presence of a ward may be safely detected through the moon's light without triggering its arcane effects."

Angelica started toward the stairwell. "Come on. It's time we found out what we're up against."

Keeping the book, I pursued her down the stairwell. Whatever trepidation I had felt about delving into questions that should remain unanswered had been overwhelmed by the exhilaration of having solved Morgaine's puzzle and the thrill of soon discovering the secrets behind the hidden door.

When we returned to the plaque bearing the symbol of Cancer, Angelica removed her crystal from her robes. I shot her a look of concern.

"Don't worry," she said. "I'm not going to summon my soul light, but we'll need something to reflect the light of the moon."

I quickly realized what she meant. The moonlight filtering through the narrow windows illuminated the floor, but without help, the light would never touch the plaque.

Angelica touched her crystal to the moonlight, which gleamed against the smooth surface. She angled the crystal toward the plaque, sending a pale ray of moonlight onto the symbol for Cancer. When the light touched the symbol, it began to shimmer, and I saw the faint outline of the sigil. In the center was the familiar triangular glyph of *Bahal Aol,* the one Una said sends out a warning to its maker. I let out a nervous breath. We would have been caught red-handed if we had triggered it with our soul light.

Another glyph was added to each side of *Bahal Aol.* Together, they appeared similar to a capital "T" that had been cut in two with *Bahal Aol* in its center.

"Do you recognize it?" Angelica asked.

"Some of it," I replied. The three symbols forming the glyph in the center trigger an alarm. It would have alerted Orionde. But I don't recognize the glyphs to each side of it."

I began searching through the *Mysteria Symbola* until I came across the severed T-shaped symbols. *"Emitges"* was the name for it. "It means 'to seal.' It's what's binding the door shut. The author says that a portal sealed with *Emitges* cannot be opened by mortal means."

Angelica swore under her breath. "So, now, what do we do? Morgain did not give me any more guidance."

"Perhaps Aqueron Lysander has a solution." I leafed through the pages. I was nearing the end of the book and beginning to lose hope when I found something on the second-to-last page. "He talks about dispelling a ward."

"What does it say?" Angelica asked, leaning over my shoulder.

As I read the words aloud, the optimism I'd felt upon finding the passage began to fade.

"The secret to dispelling a properly crafted ward remains a mystery. Of all known practitioners, only the exiled Prince Mestor has ever successfully dispelled a ward when he vanquished the one that

sealed the Sacred Vault of Atlantis and stole many of the great trea-sures for himself. Mestor's patron was Astaroth, the Grand Duke of Hell, and in the ancient writings of that demon lord, Mestor discov-ered the secret. It is believed he shared that knowledge, and the other mysteries known to Astaroth, with his most devoted disciples.

Angelica let out a long sigh. "Now what?"

I shook my head in frustration. "Let's hope one of Mestor's disciples wrote down this secret—and that the writing exists somewhere in this library."

CHAPTER 15

THE DARK SIDE
OF THE MOON

Angelica and I spent the next several hours scouring the shelves on magic and mysticism. We found nothing written by Prince Mestor, but that did not rule out writings by his disciples. The problem was we had no idea who they were.

After we retired to our chambers, I slept restlessly. My thoughts spun like wheels as I searched for a solution to the ward. My pride fueled these thoughts, for I couldn't stand a puzzle my mind couldn't solve. But alongside those thoughts was a feeling that, as exciting as this quest had become, it was wrong. The ward existed for a reason. Perhaps whatever was hidden behind that stone plaque was never meant to be found.

In the morning, I ate a light breakfast before heading outside for my lesson with Orionde. Those lessons, after all, were the reason for my apprenticeship at Rosefleur. Today's lesson focused on summoning fire, so I arrived prepared with my quarterstaff made of hard ash and blackened with soot and flaxseed oil. The staff related to an apothegm Orionde had taught me about wielding the power to control the elements:

> *Stone cuts earth, staff kindles fire.*
> *Sword parts air, cup binds water.*
> *Spirit incites the power.*

Orionde and four of her white-clad sisters, including Una, waited for me. They stood around a massive iron cauldron on the barren plain fifty yards from the tower. Flames flickered from the cauldron's opening. Glancing around, I realized Angelica wasn't among my teachers. Although she had mastered the Fae arts years ago, she often watched my lessons and sometimes joined in. However, after our late night, I suspected she had wisely chosen to rest instead.

I spent the first hour of the lesson learning the foreign-sounding words that, when arranged precisely into a verse, with the required clarity of thought, can invoke the power to summon fire. By midday, I was drawing plumes of fire from the cauldron to my staff. They gathered around my staff's tip, whirling into a fiery sphere. Then, using more words of power, I learned to hurl those fireballs at an opponent. The Fae, posing as my targets, were never in danger. With their mastery of the power, they would fling the fireballs back into the cauldron with the whisper of a word and the wave of a hand. We repeated the lesson until fatigue set in and sapped the strength from my limbs.

"Well done, Maugis," Orionde said as I bent over, hands on my knees, trying to catch my breath. "You seem to have a knack for the flame."

I flashed her a tired grin. "Does it ever get easier, fatigue-wise?"

"Somewhat," she replied. "But always remember, the

fatigue is your friend. It warns you that the power is taxing your body and acts as a signal to stop using it. To ignore the fatigue can be fatal."

"I'll remember that."

"Good," Orionde said with a nod. "Rest tomorrow. The day after next, I'll teach you new ways to use fire as a weapon."

She turned away and headed for the tower. As her sisters began to follow, I called to Una. She stopped and looked back.

"Do you have time for a question?" I asked.

"From the ever-curious Maugis d'Aygremont?" she replied with a smile. "Of course."

"Are there any books in the library written by a Prince Mestor of Atlantis? Or perhaps one of his companions?"

Una's eyes narrowed. "Where did you hear his name?"

"He's mentioned by Aqueron Lysander in the *Mysteria Symbola.*"

"Right," she sighed. "Maugis, you'd do best to forget that name. He was an evil man."

"You say that like you knew him."

She looked away briefly. "We all knew him. He was the brother of King Arcanus, and his actions ultimately led to the fall of Atlantis. He was a servant of the Dragon and had fallen in league with one of the Dragon's offspring, a powerful demon named Astaroth. Anything Mestor learned from Astaroth would be too dangerous to keep in a library. Too dangerous to keep anywhere, in fact. So, while it's true that Mestor and his disciples wrote down Astaroth's dark secrets, we spent a century after his death tracking down those writings and destroying them."

"I had no idea."

"One thing you'll learn," she said, softly touching my

shoulder, "is that some things are too dangerous to allow them to exist in this world."

I walked back to the tower with Una's words turning in my head. The same thought had kept me up half the night. For why else would Orionde have gone to such lengths to seal the secret door in the library? Yet Una claimed the writings of Mestor and his disciples had all been destroyed. If that were so, there would be no way to dispel the ward; our quest to find the hidden book seemed at an end.

Or so I thought until Angelica found me half an hour before supper. She had an excited gleam in her eyes.

"Maugis," she said, "I know how to defeat the ward."

"While you were at your lesson," Angelica explained, "I went back to the cottage. I was already tired, so it was not hard to sleep, and Morgain found me in my dreams. She told me about the astral plane, the place where she finds me in the dream world. And she taught me the secret to dispelling the ward."

She leaned in so close that her lips nearly brushed my cheek.

"We have to go back to the library tonight, Maugis. I know I can do it."

I was stunned. Had Morgain been privy to Mestor's secrets? Could she have known him in Atlantis, like Una had? The thought settled like a lump in the pit of my stomach.

Angelica locked eyes with mine. Hers shimmered with a deep yet beautiful conviction. I should have said no. Instead, I nodded, and the choice sat heavy in my chest.

I don't remember eating supper that day, but I will

never forget the growing unease I felt waiting for nightfall to meet Angelica in the library.

When the time came, we padded up the stairs to the library's third floor. As I had the night before, I brought the handheld lantern, and we used its light to locate the stone plaque on the wall bearing the symbol of Cancer.

"How do you plan to do this?" I asked.

"Morgain called it absorption, the process of using the power to draw the enchantment of the ward from the plaque into me."

I shot her a look of alarm. "You can't—"

Angelica held up a hand to silence me. "Morgain believes I'm strong enough to do it."

"Stop for a moment and think," I said sternly. "We don't know if we can trust Morgain, whoever she is. And there's a reason Orionde sealed this vault, to make sure whatever's inside it stays there."

Angelica let out a frustrated sigh. "You'd have Orionde keep us from the truth?"

"What if we're about to open Pandora's Box? Something that lets all hell into the world?"

"You don't know that," she insisted. "But we deserve to know the truth behind all these secrets. So, I'm doing this. And if you don't want me to, then back off."

I stepped back, wounded by the anger in her voice.

She stretched out her right arm as if reaching for the plaque and began reciting words unfamiliar to my ears. I felt a thrum in the air and watched as thin tendrils of energy seeped from the plaque into her open palm. As she repeated the verse, she began to grimace. The tendrils became thicker, the energy grew brighter, and the surrounding thrum became a sizzle. My mouth fell open when I saw blood-red lines crawling up her arm. The lines morphed into shapes, taking the forms of the symbols that made up the ward as if she had summoned them onto her flesh. The symbols became brighter, writhing and twisting across her skin. She stifled a cry, her expression creased with agony. I reached for her arm, hoping to pull it away, but when my fingers touched her skin, my hand recoiled as if I had grasped hot iron. Angelica dropped to a knee, her entire body shaking as the shifting symbols settled into her arm, growing darker like dried blood.

Then, in a breath, it was over. Angelica stood, sweat beading on her forehead, and touched the plaque. It slid inward on the right side. With a scrape of stone, she pulled the plaque free from the wall, revealing a dark hollow.

"You ... did it," I said breathlessly, horrified by the symbols tattooed on her right arm.

With a groan, she reached in and drew something from the hollow. It was a book bound in weathered, dark leather. In the flickering lantern light, fading symbols on the book's surface seemed to dance and shift. Cradling the book with both hands, Angelica cracked open the cover.

I swear I heard the book speak a word, subtle like a serpent's hiss.

"Yes ..."

CHAPTER 16

INTERLUDE

"How very clever," Nimue said.

She sat on a stool, a pewter flute of wine in her hand. Maugis had been so absorbed in telling her the story that he had no idea where the stool or the flute had come from.

In his right ear came a clicking chatter. Out of the corner of his eye, he glimpsed two of the glossy white spiders, their legs whispering across the massive web that held him fast, their sixteen black eyes glittering like pits of ink. One of them paused, tilting its head, as if listening.

"It appears Morgain chose wisely with this Angelica," Nimue went on. "She seems remarkable. And terribly determined. The only mortal I'd ever known to attempt to absorb a ward like that was Mestor himself."

"Mestor?" Maugis croaked. "You knew him, back in Atlantis."

Nimue sipped her wine, then licked a red droplet from her smooth lips. "We all knew him. He was handsome, ambitious, and ruthless, but not uncharming. He was much more fun than his brother. Arcanus was always so serious, much like I suspect you are, Maugis d'Aygremont. Orionde likes that type."

Her gaze flicked toward him, amused.

"But Angelica, she's something different, isn't she?" Nimue leaned forward, her voice almost a whisper. "I would very much like to meet her."

Maugis grimaced. Her words reopened a wound, one so deep it tormented him to think about.

Nimue swirled her wine lazily, as if this were a fireside chat rather than his torture. "Tell me the rest."

He did not want to. He could not bear it. But the elixer she had fed him slithered through his mind, pulling at the seams of his will. As hard as he tried to resist, his tongue moved of its own accord.

"Angelica …"

CHAPTER 17

ALL HALLOWS EVE

Angelica spent the next day locked away in her chamber. She would not see me. Whether it was anger at my attempt to stop her or exhaustion from dispelling the ward, I couldn't say. I only knew the silence unsettled me. Yet to my relief, she came to me the next day, after my lesson with Orionde.

I was in the tower's scriptorium, a long, narrow chamber that followed the curve of the tower one floor above the library. Beneath a barrel-vaulted ceiling, an array of archways stretched the length of the scriptorium, each one framing an alcove with a window and a finely carved writing desk. My desk was tucked away in an alcove at the farthest end of the chamber, and I sat there, writing down everything I had learned during my lesson. When I heard footsteps on the stone floor, I set down my quill and turned my head. Angelica was walking toward my alcove, barefoot, wearing a white dress with long sleeves. Her face looked paler than usual, and I noticed a hint of dark circles beneath her eyes.

I stood up from my desk. "Are you all right?"

"Yes," she replied, running a hand through her raven hair. "I've been studying the book."

That explained her tired look.

"Can you tell who wrote it?" I asked.

"The author's name is not mentioned."

That was odd. "What have you found?"

"It tells how to use the power in ways I've never imagined, things we've never been taught. Some parts are disturbing." She hesitated, her gaze dropping to the floor. "But haven't we learned that the power itself is not good or evil? It's how one uses it that makes it so."

"Right," I said. That was what we'd been taught, but after learning about Prince Mestor, I had my doubts.

She held my hands; her skin was cold to the touch.

"I discovered how to save her," Angelica continued. "The book contains instructions to open a gateway to the deeper reaches of the Otherworld, and describes the words of power to draw forth beings who are imprisoned there. Tomorrow is All Hallows Eve, when the barrier between worlds will be at its thinnest. It will be the ideal time to free her, and I know I can do it."

"Are you sure this is right?" I asked, though the question made my stomach clench. "Something about this feels wrong."

She squeezed my hands. "You haven't felt her suffering like I have. I have to save her, Maugis, and I want you with me when I do it."

She leaned forward; her lips touched my cheek. "Promise me you'll help?"

I thought of turning away, but she placed a hand behind my head and drew me to her lips. One kiss turned into two, and more. Her hand dropped to my waist, and in the time it took to sharpen a quill, we gave ourselves to one another on my desk. Never had we been so reckless within the tower's walls. But the strange chill of her skin mixing with the heat of our passion created a sensation I could not resist.

By the time we were finished, I would have done anything for her. No matter what my conscience was telling me.

The next evening was All Hallows Eve. The barriers between worlds were beginning to fray. You could almost feel it in the air around Rosefleur.

So I went with Angelica to free Morgain.

And nothing would ever be the same.

THE BORDER of what the Fae called the Riverlands was a mile west of Rosefleur. We set out hours after sunset. Our trek across the barren plain would have been in total darkness if not for the faint moonlight seeping in from the mortal world. Our breath froze in the cold air.

The mountains were the first sign we were nearing the border. They rose into the darkness, towering, jagged crags of rock that, like the forest, formed a wall around this portion of the plain. The base of the mountains was awash in a pale glow, a telltale sign that we were approaching the water. The glow came from the Lethe, which had formed a crescent-shaped lake at the foot of the mountain. The river itself must have run through an underground tunnel, for the glowing water emanated from a massive cave opening that resembled the mouth of a yawning giant. As far as I knew, the Fae had never built a boat to traverse the waters from the shore to the cave. And the reason for that was clear: Wherever the water came from, no one was meant to go there.

When we reached the lakeshore, Angelica removed the

black-bound book from a satchel slung over her shoulder. The sight of the tome sent a wave of unease through my stomach.

"What are you going to do now?" I asked her.

"Morgain told me about a barrier between the land surrounding Rosefleur and the place where she's imprisoned. The barrier's invisible, but it's at the mouth of the cave. I'm going to weaken it and draw her through."

As she reached to open the book, I noticed the blood-red symbols tattooed on the skin of her right arm between her wrist and the hem of her sleeve.

She leafed through the pages, and in the glow emanating from the lake, I caught a glimpse of the writing. The ink was brown with age, and the script was inscribed with a meticulous, almost obsessive hand. Interspersed within the text were diagrams and illustrations, reminding me of my own journal. But where my drawings were the work of an apprentice, whoever made this book was an absolute master.

"You might want to stand back," she said, her eyes unafraid and filled with determination.

I took a step back as she began reciting the incantation. I sensed a crackle in the air. The verse flowed off her lips like a song. I understood some of the words, but most were foreign to me, punctuated with a name spoken over and over. *"Morgain."*

She reached an arm toward the cave, and the symbols on her arm flared brighter. As she repeated the verse, her outstretched arm began to shake, and veins bulged in her neck. Her voice rose, and I felt a tremor in the earth beneath my feet. Then, a spark burst within the darkness of the cave. A roar filled my ears as something shot towards us like an arrow, skimming over the surface of the water, throwing up a wake of glowing spray followed by billowing clouds of steam.

Angelica dropped the book and staggered backward.

I darted to my right, for the object was speeding straight toward us. I heard a scream, and the next thing I knew, a body struck the shore, blasting forth a torrent of glowing liquid before skidding to a halt on the damp ground. The figure was as large as one of the Fae, long-legged, barefoot, and wearing a tattered dress stained black with grime. A tangle of long, black hair, wet and shimmering like polished obsidian, spilled down her back. She lay there, head down and unmoving, while tendrils of steam wafted from her body.

Breathless and wide-eyed, Angelica turned to the figure.

"Morgain?"

CHAPTER 18

ACCOLON

"Morgain?" Angelica asked again, a hint of fear in her voice.

The woman did not move.

"Let's turn her over," I suggested. I knelt down and put a hand on her shoulder. Her body was hot to the touch. Gently, I turned her over.

Her face, like so many of the Fae, was ageless with sculpted cheekbones and alabaster skin. Her eyes were closed beneath delicately curved eyebrows, the same obsidian black as her dripping-wet hair.

"Can you hear us?" Angelica whispered.

The woman's eyelids sprang open.

Before I could react, her hand shot toward my throat, fingers clamping down like iron. My breath vanished. Then, with effortless force, she hurled me ten paces away.

I hit the ground hard; Angelica gasped.

Morgain rose to her feet in a single, fluid motion. As tall as Una, she glanced between us, her gaze settling on Angelica. "Angelica?"

"I'm here," Angelica said softly.

Morgain turned to me, her face bathed in the lake's eerie glow. Her emerald-green eyes, flaring at first, began to soften. "I'm … sorry," she murmured.

I picked myself off the ground, eying her warily. There was no malice in her expression. Still, I kept a hand an inch from the hilt of the dagger sheathed at my belt.

"Are you Morgain?" Angelica asked.

"Yes, child," the woman said. She scratched the side of her head as if thinking. "Can you take me to my cottage?"

Angelica nodded before bending down and retrieving the black-bound book.

The ghost of a smile touched Morgain's lips. "The *Book of Shadows*, I knew you'd find it."

A chill ran down my spine at the name. *The Book of Shadows?*

Angelica returned the book to her satchel, and the three of us set off. The cottage stood on the other side of the land surrounding Rosefleur, several miles from the lake. We walked for more than an hour around the perimeter of the forest, speaking little. Angelica looked as wary as I felt, but she followed Morgain as if she were eager to learn the answer to the mystery that had consumed our week.

When we reached the curtain of mist, Angelica reached for her crystal, but Morgain touched her forearm. "Allow me," she said.

Morgain stretched out her right arm and spoke a word. *"Eoh."*

Eldritch blue light burst from her fingertips, and the curtain of mist parted as if blasted by a gale. If I had any lingering doubts about whether Morgain was one of the Fae, that act dispelled them.

Upon reaching our destination, Morgain stopped to gaze upon the cottage. "My home," she said, her eyes welling with emotion.

We followed her inside into complete darkness. Morgain spoke the word again, and a halo of light ignited in the palm of her left hand. Slowly, she looked around until her gaze settled on the sigil carved into the wall above the bed. She ran the fingers of her right hand over the symbols.

"This was my beacon," she said, her voice barely above a whisper. "It's what allowed me to reach you through the astral plane."

"How long ago did you live here?" Angelica asked.

Morgain shook her head, her brow furrowing as if grasping at a memory. "More than twenty years ago," she finally said.

I glanced at the sigil where the name "MORGAIN" formed half a circle above the word "ACCOLON."

"Who was Accolon?" I asked.

Morgain inhaled sharply, her fingers trailing over the carved letters. "He was a chevalier under the Prince of the Franks, Charles Martel. He fought with him in the great battle that saved your lands from the Moors and sent them back to their caliphate."

I nodded. My own father had fought in the Battle of Tours alongside my king's grandfather, the one they called Charles the Hammer.

"When he was not fighting for the prince," Morgain went on, "Accolon used to hunt in these woods. That is how we met. I have known many great men over the centuries, but Accolon might have been the finest among them. In time, we grew close. He understood what I was and why I could not leave here, so we would meet at this cottage when he was not off at court or in battle. It was our hideaway."

"You are one of the Sisters of Orionde?" I asked.

Morgain scoffed at that. "Orionde was not always our

leader. But you are correct. I was among those you call the Fae who left Avalon for Rosefleur more than a hundred years ago. I am not surprised they no longer speak my name."

So Una had been lying, I thought. *She knew Morgain, they were sisters. But why would she lie?*

"What happened to you and Accolon?" Angelica asked.

Any trace of a smile vanished from Morgain's face. "Love between your kind and mine is forbidden, nature be damned. But we were unwilling to lock away our feelings and accept the pain of being apart. We had made something together, something more precious than anything Orionde and our sisters could ever comprehend. Perhaps they were jealous or spite-filled, or maybe they were simply hellbent on enforcing their senseless rules. One day, we were betrayed and discovered. Accolon was filled with righteous anger; he was never one to back down. He risked everything to protect the life we had made together. He drew his blade on Orionde, and without an ounce of mercy, she killed him."

Angelica's hands flew to her lips; I sucked in a startled breath.

As she spoke, the glow in Morgain's left palm flickered, shrinking like a dying ember. Shadows deepened around us.

"I was arrested and taken to the place where you summoned me. There, Orionde rendered her judgment. I was banished deep into the Riverlands. A land others call Hades or Sheol. For years, I lingered in its oppressive gloom until you reached me through this sigil and brought me home."

Listening to her, I felt a pang of sympathy. But part of her story seemed wrong, for I found it hard to imagine

Orionde willing a man's death. Yet had she not wished the same fate on Charles's brother Carloman? My head ached with the thought.

I glanced at Angelica, who seemed captivated by Morgain's tale.

"I can't imagine how awful this must have been for you," Angelica said. "How can we help?"

Morgain gestured to her tattered, filthy dress. "You could find me some new clothes. And I have not had good food or drink since I entered that hellish prison."

Angelica gave her a nod. "In the morning, I will bring them to you."

"That would be good of you," Morgain replied. "I must ask, does Orionde know you've had contact with me? Or has she seemed suspicious of your affairs?"

"No." Angelica shook her head. "I've never spoken to her about you, and she pays little mind to where I go and what I do. She only cares about her new apprentice, Maugis."

Morgain raised a brow, then fixed her gaze on me. "Does Orionde suspect *you* know about me?"

"I can't imagine how she would," I said defensively, without mentioning that I had asked Una about her. *Though would Una have told Orionde?*

"It must stay that way," Morgain said sternly, cutting off my thoughts. "I do not believe she knows of this cottage. When she confronted Accolon and me, we were in a glade two miles from here. I'm certain that if she had known about this place, she would have burned it to the ground. And if she were to learn of my return now, she and her followers would send me back to where they banished me. Or worse, try to destroy me once and for all."

"I swear," Angelica said, "we will keep this secret."

I did not like the thought of keeping secrets from Orionde, and I felt relieved when it seemed we might leave Morgain and return to Rosefleur. It had to be well past midnight. However, before we departed, I felt compelled to ask Morgain one final question: "What will you do now?"

She thought for a moment until the hint of a smile appeared on her lips.

"I'm going to find a way to take back everything I've lost."

CHAPTER 19

THE BOOK OF SHADOWS

By the time we passed through the misty barrier and returned to the barren plain surrounding Rose-fleur, the air had grown frigid, but Angelica was burning with indignation.

"The hypocrisy of it all is galling," she huffed. "There are scores of stories about Faerie women luring men into their lairs. How do you think those stories came to be? This isn't the first time one of the Fae has taken a mortal lover. It's the bloody reason they came here in the first place. Yet Orionde *banished* Morgain to some version of hell for this indiscretion, and, if that were not terrible enough, she *killed* Accolon."

"Morgain said it was Accolon who first drew his blade," I reminded her. "If Orionde killed him, perhaps it was in defense."

Angelica threw up her hands. "Or maybe she just wanted him gone, and killing him was the surest way to make that happen. That's how she is, you know."

"That's not true," I insisted.

"Maugis, I've known her my entire life. When Orionde

perceives an obstacle to her desires, she *eliminates* it. Just like she did with your father and brother, in case you've forgotten."

Those words stopped me in my tracks.

Was it true? Orionde had lured my father to his death during a hunt, but it was his lust for her that drove him into the trap. She had also driven Vivian to Rosefleur, but the only reason he went there was to kill me and claim Aygremont for his own. But I *was* the one who summoned Bayard to stop him.

I was the one who killed him.

Yet Orionde arranged for all of it to happen, all to have me as her apprentice. And she'd have me do the same to Charles's brother.

I tipped my head toward the starless sky and sighed. "Maybe you're right."

Yet, nothing about this felt right. There had to be a missing piece to this puzzle.

I just needed to find it.

I WOKE up to a knock on my door. I did not know how long I had slept, but pale sunlight shone through a narrow window of leaded glass.

"Maugis, are you in there?" a voice called through the door. I recognized it as Una's. "You're going to miss your lesson."

I scratched my head. The lesson wasn't supposed to begin until midday. Had I slept so long? I pulled on my breaches, walked bare-chested to the door, and opened it.

Una stood there with her coppery curls cascading over her shoulders. She looked me up and down with a wry smile on her lips. "Whatever were you doing last night? You missed breakfast, which is *very* unlike you."

She handed me an apple.

"Sorry," I said, taking it. "I don't know why I slept so long."

"Well, I suppose you'll be rested for your lesson. We'll be working with the wind, and we've brought out Archimedes."

"Right," I said with a nod. "I'll be right down."

"Don't be late," she urged with a brightness in her eyes before heading for the stairwell.

I closed the door and took a bite of the apple, trying to imagine what today's lesson would entail. Archimedes was the name of an elaborate kite about the size of a hog built to look vaguely like an owl. It was named after a real owl that had belonged to Merlin, one of their former apprentices. The kite was composed of a light wooden frame with large sheets of parchment covering its broad wings, small head, and barrel-shaped torso. The whole thing weighed less than a sheepdog, and using the wind, one could make it fly.

After finishing the apple, I put on my boots and sable tunic, followed by my sable cloak fastened with a leopard-shaped brooch, and then my belt strapped to the scabbard holding my leaf-shaped blade. I quickly combed my hair with my fingers and headed for my lesson.

Archimedes was sitting where the cauldron had been days ago, fifty yards from the tower. Standing around him were Orionde and Una, two of the golden-haired Fae— Theia and Pandeia—and Raina, with her braided platinum hair piled high on her head. Angelica was nowhere to be seen, and I suspected she had returned to the cottage with the things Morgain had asked for. My stomach clenched at the thought. A good night's sleep had done nothing to ease my concern about our mysterious Morgain.

"Maugis," Orionde said, "It's so good of you to join us. Today's lesson will test both your skill and endurance. We're going to see how long you can keep Archimedes in the air. Remember, fatigue is your friend. When you begin to feel tired, land Archimedes gently on the ground, and we'll discuss what you've learned."

"Yes, My Lady," I replied before drawing my sword and readying myself. I cleared my mind and began moving the sword in a circular motion while reciting the words to summon the wind. When I felt the air whirling around my sword arm, I directed it toward Archimedes and uttered more words to send the wind into a skyward gale. The wind lifted the artificial owl off the ground, and soon, it was gliding through the air like a bird of prey. I added more verses to the melody that kept Archimedes aloft, causing the owl to swoop and rise as it circled overhead, all the while moving my sword like a general directing troops in battle. Every few minutes, one of my instructors would launch a blast of wind at the owl, forcing me to concentrate harder to keep control of it. After a time, I learned to make Archimedes dodge these attacks, soaring above the blasts of wind or plummeting beneath them before elevating to circle our outdoor classroom.

Eventually, my sword arm began to ache, but the rest of me felt fine, so I kept going. Then, suddenly, I felt Archimedes pull hard against my will. I worried I had flown him into one of my instructor's traps as I fought to maintain control. Grimacing, I uttered another verse, but Archimedes broke free and, to my horror, dove straight toward Orionde.

The wind behind the owl howled as it sped forward. Gasps erupted around me, and a cry stuck in my throat.

Just as it seemed Archimedes would crash into Orionde, she leaped aside. Archimedes struck the ground with a shuddering boom, its wooden frame exploding into pieces as parchment tore and its wings went flying.

"Liar!" a voice screamed.

I looked toward the sound. Angelica, her face full of fury, gripped her leaf-shaped blade while astride one of the roan mares. With all my attention on Archimedes, I hadn't even noticed her approach. But I was sure she was the one who took control of the owl and sent it rushing toward Orionde.

"You're all liars and deceivers!" Angelica pointed her sword at Una. "You are a betrayer," she yelled before leveling the blade at Orionde. "And you are a murderer!"

"Angelica!" Orionde shouted back. "What is the meaning of this!"

"You all knew," Angelica cried, "For twenty-two years, you knew. Yet not one of you said a goddamned thing!"

The color drained from Orionde's face while Una and her sisters stood stunned.

"Rosefleur is not my home, and you are not my family." Angelica sheathed her sword and grabbed the mare's reins with both hands. "All of you belong in hell!"

Then she wheeled her mount and rode off at a furious pace.

My mouth hung open as I watched her head for the forest. The next thing I knew, someone grabbed my left arm in a steel grip.

"What has happened?" Orionde demanded, anger flickering in her eyes.

Looking at her, a sudden coldness settled deep within my core. "We learned of a woman—Morgain—and Angelica freed her."

Orionde's eyes widened; her hand slid off my arm and fell limp by her side.

"What?"

I told her about the cottage, the sigils, the names carved into the wall, and Angelica's dreams.

"How did she free her?" Orionde asked in a bewildered tone.

"There was a book … hidden in the library. Through her dreams, Morgain told her how to find it. I helped her," I admitted, overwhelmed with shame. "Angelica used it to free Morgain at the lakeshore. Morgain called it the *Book of Shadows*."

One of the sisters gasped; Orionde staggered back.

"You foolish, reckless child," Orionde said, her voice on the verge of rage, "you have no idea what you've done. That book was written by Astaroth, a scion of the Dragon!"

Her words struck me like a blow.

"Why did you have it?" I cried out. "Why didn't you destroy it?"

"We tried, but it cannot be destroyed!"

A surge of panic pulsed through my veins. "What do we do now?"

Orionde's expression hardened like stone.

"We have to stop her before something terrible happens."

CHAPTER 20
THE GLAMOUR

That afternoon, Orionde and all seventeen of her sister Fae set out for the cottage. The Fae were fully armed, mounted on chargers, and clad in close-fitting hauberks of shining silver scale mail. At Orionde's insistence, I led the way astride Bayard.

We rode at a gallop, and the thunder of hooves drowned out all other sounds, but it did nothing to quell the questions assailing my mind. What lies had Angelica been told that drove her into this rage? I had never seen her so furious and reckless, and I could not help but believe she had been influenced by Morgain and the *Book of Shadows*. And if that book *was* written by one of the Dragon's offspring, as Orionde had claimed, then we had indeed opened Pandora's Box, and who knew what evil we had let into the world?

The dread within me grew as we charged into the forest. Bayard knew his way through the maze of trees and brambles like no other, and he kept his furious pace. When the curtain of mist emerged between the trees, I heard Orionde utter a word behind me, and with a blast of soul light, the curtain parted, and we entered Francia. I was suddenly overwhelmed by the odor of burning wood a moment before I saw the smoke, black and billowing through the trees. Next, I heard the crackle of flames, and my heart began pounding with fear. I spurred Bayard deeper into the woods and started screaming when I saw the cottage had become an inferno.

"Angelica! Angelica!"

I leapt off Bayard's back and started for the cottage despite the flames raging ten feet high.

"Maugis, back away!" I heard Una cry.

The heat made me retreat a step. Then I heard a verse, and the air around me thrummed. The roaring fire began to subside until the burnt walls held the glow of embers, and wisps of smoke hissed off its surface. The Fae were controlling the flames now, so without a second thought, I rushed inside, hollering, "Angelica!"

Inside, the cottage felt like an oven. The bed was destroyed, covered in ash, and the sigil that once adorned the wall was blackened by soot. But my worst fear—a body burned beyond recognition—was not realized. The cottage was empty.

I ducked out the door, yelling frantically, "Angelica!"

No one answered. Then, with a loud woosh, the Fae released control of the fire, and the blaze erupted, rocketing to a column of flame fifty feet high. The flames settled into a bonfire, consuming the cottage, but by then, I had mounted Bayard. With a barely parting glance, I charged off into the woods to find Angelica.

"Maugis, wait!" I heard Una cry behind me.

"Let him go," another voice said harshly. It was Orionde's.

By now, my heart was racing, and fear drowned out all reason. Had they tried, I would have done anything to prevent them from stopping me. Yet no one followed as I drove Bayard deeper into the forest.

I searched everywhere we had ever gone together in the woods until the sun went down, and long after that. But I did not find her. I'd lost track of the Fae, though I wondered if they, too, had set off to scour the forest. I did not know what hour of the night it was by the time Bayard and I returned to the curtain of mist. I infused the gemstone set into my ring with soul light and traversed the mists safely back into the Otherworld. When I reached the tower, I stabled Bayard and discovered the rest of the Fae's mounts already there. Then I climbed the stairway to my chamber, exhausted from my fruitless search.

I unpinned the brooch that held my cloak in place and let it fall to the ground. My chamber was dark, save for the faint moonlight seeping through the narrow window. I inhaled a scent like cinnamon that made me feel slightly lightheaded before I realized I was not alone in the room.

"Maugis," Angelica said softly.

She stepped into the moonlight, wearing a sleeveless white shift of thin cloth, the fabric clinging to her form. Down her right arm, dark red runes twisted like serpents. Her green eyes were wide, filled with something I couldn't name.

Love? Desire?

I wrapped her in an embrace, inhaling more of the cinnamon scent. Her hair was thick with the smell. My limbs tingled. A pleasant numbness crept through me, like the slow pull of wine.

"What is happening?" I whispered.

"Just hold me, Maugis," she said before kissing my earlobe.

A shiver rolled down my spine. Heat coiled below my waist, spreading like fire. Her lips pressed against mine, and whatever thoughts lingered, whatever doubts I might have had, vanished in the sweetness of her scent. My pulse pounded. My body ached for her. And she was more than willing to give herself to me.

Our passion that night reached heights I had never before experienced. It was raw, wild, wondrous.

When we were finished, I fell asleep holding her in my arms.

But hours later, when I woke, something felt … wrong.

The scent had changed. No longer cinnamon, but something colder, something floral and strange. The body in my arms felt different, unfamiliar. Slowly, I opened my eyes.

The woman lying naked next to me was not Angelica.
It was Morgain.

I jumped up, my head pounding as if I had drunk two skins of wine the night before.

"Why are you here?"

Covering herself with a sheet, Morgain got out of bed. "Because I needed to keep you occupied."

"I wasn't with you last night," I insisted.

"It's called a glamour, Maugis, a convincing illusion. You only thought you were with Angelica, though my perfume, brewed to dampen a man's wits and inflame his desires, aided in the deception."

I could not believe what I was hearing. "Why did you do this?"

"Because I needed to buy her time," she said with a cunning look. "I've already told you that."

A sickness churned in my stomach. "Time for what?"

"Time for her to finish the ritual, to achieve our vengeance."

A cold fury rose in me. "Vengeance? What have you done to her mind?"

Morgain tilted her head, as if amused by my anger. "I told her the truth," she said. "The truth everyone here has kept from her all these years. It awakened something inside her. And I can assure you, she will not be denied."

I crawled out of bed, my hands balled into fists. "What are you talking about?"

Morgain narrowed her gaze. "The reason Accolon died." She paused, letting her words sink in.

"I told you he had risked everything to protect the life we had made. Well, that life was our daughter—Angelica."

The breath left my lungs.

"They killed him," Morgain continued, her voice thickening with anger. "Then banished me, and took her for themselves, never telling her the truth about who she was or where she came from. And now, they'll pay for their sins."

A wave of nausea crashed over me. I staggered forward, hands bracing against the bedpost, and then I wretched, emptying my stomach onto the floor.

Behind me, the sheet fluttered to the ground as Morgain rose and strode barefoot toward the door.

She paused, glancing back at me over her shoulder.

"It's over, Maugis. The die has been cast, and there's nothing you can do to stop it."

CHAPTER 21

REVENGE

I staggered to my feet, gripping the bedpost as the world tilted around me. My breath came fast, my mind reeling.

Her daughter …

As stunning as that realization was, it suddenly all made sense. Angelica had been raised at Rosefleur since she was a small child, with no memory of her parents. I could only imagine her shock and rage upon learning that the Fae had killed her father, banished her mother, and kept this secret from her for her entire life. But now, what had she done? What ritual had she performed in the name of vengeance?

Trying to ignore my growing dread, I yanked on my breeches, pulled on my boots, and threw my sable tunic over my head. My thoughts were racing faster than my hands. The only other thing I thought to take was my swordbelt, which held my leaf-shaped blade sheathed in its scabbard. I secured it around my waist, the familiar weight settling against my hip.

Then I stepped out into the passageway.

The first thing I noticed was the fog. Wisps of violet vapor lingered in the passageway, carrying the earthy scent of poppy flowers. For a moment, I worried about the effect this substance might have on me, but besides its scent, it was no different than a damp evening mist.

The violet fog thickened as I descended the curved stairway leading to the scriptorium. Through the haze, I saw the first of them sprawled on the ground.

Thalia.

She lay unmoving, her silvery hair spilling wildly around her head. My heart sank. I bent down and touched her. Her skin was cold. I shook her gently, dread curling in my gut. She didn't wake.

I felt a chill of fear. Then, faint, against my fingertips, I felt a breath. She was alive, but would not wake.

Relief shuddered through me, but it did little to push back my increasing alarm. I rose and moved faster, descending into the library. Violet fog curled through the shelves like living mist. I searched each floor, half-expecting to find Una unconscious among the books, but the library stood empty. The silence clawed at my nerves.

I moved to the garden and froze.

Surrounded by the violet fog, three of the Fae had collapsed around the fountain. My instructor, Raina, lay among them. I bent to wake her, but like Thalia, she remained locked in some unnatural sleep.

I searched frantically, moving downward through the tower.

In the kitchen and refectory, I found five more. Two of them were my instructors, Theia and Pandeia. In the main hall, four more lay unconscious. In the stables, the stable master Epona and the pale-haired Selene lay motionless. But the horses, even Bayard, stood untouched by the fog's spell.

From there, I descended to the well chamber, where the water from the Lethe was purified for use in the tower. The water master, Melusine, lay beside the well, the violet mist swirling around her. That's when it struck me—two of the Fae were missing.

Una and Orionde.

My heart pounded as I whirled around. I raced up the tower, searching every floor, lungs burning with every step.

I could not find them.

I reached the upper gallery atop Rosefleur, gasping for breath. The vaulted chamber was empty save for wisps of violet fog, shimmering in the faint light leaking through the towering windows.

What had she done to them?

I glanced outside. Beyond the tower, Rosefleur's barren plain stretched toward jagged mountains, aglow in the light of the Lethe pooling in the lake. At the sight of it, Angelica's accusations flooded my mind.

"You are a betrayer!" she had yelled at Una.

"And you are a murderer!" she had screamed at Orionde.

The answer slammed into me like a blow.

She was going to banish them.

A fresh wave of terror surged through me. I turned and sprinted for the stables. As I hurtled down the stairs, I prayed to whatever saint might be listening.

Just let me reach them in time.

I URGED Bayard into a furious gallop beneath the dull gray sky, racing toward the lake. In the mountain's shadow, I spotted two horses and two figures standing by the shore, their silhouettes illuminated by the Lethe's eerie glow.

"Bayard!" I shouted, twitching the reins. "Ride like the wind!"

The powerful bay stallion surged forward, his hooves pounding the earth. Wind lashed against my face as my heart thundered in my chest.

A hundred yards away, the scene on the shore sharpened into focus.

Angelica stood motionless, her head bowed, whispering words I couldn't hear. The object in her arms shimmered with a strange, pulsating glow, and I swore I could feel its power in the very air. Near her feet, an eldritch blue light flickered over two unmoving figures. Ten paces away, Morgain observed the ritual in silent satisfaction, while their horses pawed nervously at the ground.

Beyond them, across the glowing lake, the mountain loomed, its yawning cave mouth like the gaping maw of some titanic earth god, yearning for the sacrifice Angelica was preparing.

I unsheathed my sword and began whispering a verse to summon the wind. The air around me sizzled with power. Bayard's pace quickened, the world blurring past as I reached them in a breath. Air swirled around my leaf-shaped blade as I directed the wind at the object in Angelica's hands.

The Book of Shadows.

The sudden gale tore it from her grasp. It flipped wildly through the air, and I willed the wind to fling it into the lake. But to my surprise, I felt a force pushing back against my power, bending the wind away from the glowing waters, as if the book had a will of its own. It tumbled through the air once more and landed safely on the ground twenty feet from Angelica.

Angelica spun toward me. Her eyes blazed with fury.

"Angelica, stop this!" I yanked hard on Bayard's reins,

barely keeping in my saddle. "You don't have to do this. Revenge won't undo what they did to you!"

"You don't understand, Maugis," she said, her gaze locked on mine. Her lips trembled; then she drew in a breath. "They took *everything* from me."

I glanced at Una and Orionde lying asleep on the ground, wreathed in a ghostly blue light. It flickered unnaturally, curling around them.

My stomach tightened. "There has to be a better way!"

"Some sins can't be forgiven," she said, her voice now as cold as iron. Without a parting glance, she strode toward the book.

Before I could spur Bayard to follow her, a windblast struck me with the force of a battering ram. The stallion reared, nearly toppling over, while I was hurled from the saddle. I slammed into the ground, the air torn from my lungs. Pain exploded through my limbs as I rolled across the packed earth.

Gritting my teeth, I tried to scramble to my feet, only for another blast to send me flailing backward. My limbs felt weightless, useless, as I was flung like a rag doll.

I twisted my head, catching a glimpse of my attacker. *Morgain.*

She stood with arms outstretched, dark hair whipping in the storm she conjured. The wind bent to her will, and she wielded it effortlessly while I fought just to stay on my feet.

"I won't let you stop her!" Morgain shouted, her voice cutting through the howling gale.

I clawed at the cracked ground, my fingers digging into a deep groove to anchor myself. My sword lay nearly out of reach. I lunged for it. Stretching my fingers, I touched the hilt, just enough to pull it into my grasp a split second before the next blast struck.

The force wrenched my hand free, sending me into a barrel roll over the hard-packed earth. But this time, I didn't let go of my blade.

Angelica retrieved the book and resumed uttering a verse. A low, thrumming vibration rippled through the air. The eldritch flames around Orionde and Una flared brighter.

I gritted my teeth and began reciting a verse of my own.

Morgain's next windblast roared toward me, but I was ready. I swung my sword, the wind spiraling around my blade as I sent my own blast to meet hers. The two forces collided with a deafening roar. Dust and loose stones exploded into the air. The very ground seemed to tremble beneath me as I fought against her, struggling to stay upright in the howling storm.

But I knew I could not defeat her. Wielding the power was effortless for the Fae. For me, exhaustion would come soon. And when it did, I would fall.

Angelica's verse rose to a crescendo. I watched in horror as her dark magic lifted Orionde and Una two feet off the ground. Their backs arched at the waist, their arms dangling, their fingertips still brushing the desolate plain.

My arms quivered. Morgain's windblast was relentless, pressing against me like the weight of a storm. I sucked in a breath. I knew I couldn't win, but I wasn't ready to lose.

With a roar, I poured every last ounce of my will into one final thrust in the battle of winds. My blast sent Morgain staggering back, her windstorm fading. Then I bolted toward Orionde. I leaped, reaching out just as the ghostly blue flames surged around us.

I caught Orionde's arm, cold as ice beneath my hand. For a heartbeat, I feared she wouldn't wake. Then her fingers clamped onto my tunic in a desperate grip.

Before I could take another breath, Angelica's voice rang out like a thunderclap.

"Begone!"

A deafening roar shattered the air. The world cracked apart. A force beyond reckoning struck me, tearing me from the ground. My stomach lurched as we were hurled backward across the glowing lake, into the gaping maw of the cave.

Where we plunged into darkness.

CHAPTER 22

BANISHMENT

From the darkness, we burst into light, sucked deep into the Otherworld by an irresistible force. We shot over a glowing river, barely two feet above the water, into a valley flanked by towering basalt cliffs. I clung to Orionde as tightly as I could. She gripped my tunic, and Una was there, as if the ghostly blue aura binding us together refused to let us separate.

The roaring in my ears wouldn't cease as we sped through the valley beneath an endless twilight sky devoid of stars or a moon. We moved so fast that the ground blurred to gray streaks beneath us. A fiery glow pierced the gloom ahead. My breath caught as I realized we were streaking toward a wall of fire.

"Orionde!"

We punched through the flames, and the world became an inferno. Heat lashed my skin like a thousand burning needles. My lungs seized, filled with scorching air. Then, suddenly, we were falling.

I hit the ground hard, the impact ripping Orionde from my grasp. Pain exploded through me as I tumbled, stones cutting into my flesh. My tunic burned. Fire licked at my skin. I threw myself onto the dirt, rolling wildly, choking on the acrid stench of charred fabric and singed hair. I smothered the flames, but fresh pain lanced through my limbs.

Blood was streaming down my arms, trickling from raw scrapes where the fire and earth had torn at me. My breeches were shredded, and my tunic hung in blackened tatters.

"Maugis," a voice called.

I lifted my head, barely able to focus. Orionde was crawling toward me, her white dress torn and blackened from the fire. Yet, though her skin was reddened in places, she looked otherwise unscathed.

"Let me help you, or you'll bleed to death."

She whispered a word, *"Eoh,"* and bathed me in the warmth of her soul light. A tingling sensation spread through me, the raw sting of my wounds dulling into something more bearable. She moved methodically, tending to every scrape, every laceration, her touch cool and careful. My pain eased, but the deep aches in my muscles still lingered.

"Where are we?" I rasped.

"We are in the Riverlands," she replied grimly, "trapped in a valley beyond Phlegethon, the River of Fire."

I glanced over my shoulder, noticing the crackling sound for the first time now that the roaring in my ears had faded. Fifty yards away, a river barred our path. Not one of water, but of fire, an eight-foot-high inferno. The surrounding valley was bleak and unforgiving. To my left and right, jagged basalt cliffs loomed, their dark surfaces broken by deep, hollow caves that swallowed the light. Beyond them, the land stretched endlessly into the twilight.

I sat up, rubbing my throbbing limbs. Una, now awake, staggered toward us. Her coppery curls were a wild mess, her soft, pale skin streaked with soot.

"Maugis," she said, "thank God you're here."

"So we can be trapped here together?" I asked, confused by her apparent elation.

"No," Una said. "Because you're the only one who can save us."

"How?"

"Because you are mortal," she said, "and we are not."

I scratched my head, which ached almost as much as the rest of me. I could not imagine how being mortal was a blessing in this forsaken land.

"What Una means," Orionde explained, "is that the banishment spell that sent us here was designed to bind our kind, not yours. As was the spell Angelica cast before that, the one that put us into the Sleep. You are mortal, so it could not affect you."

"I don't understand."

Orionde's expression was unreadable. "Immortality comes with its burdens, Maugis. To cope with living forever, all of our kind eventually go into the Sleep. Sometimes, it lasts months; other times, years or even centuries. It soothes our minds, calms our spirits, and we awaken invigorated for the next eon of our existence. Angelica's spell forced us into the Sleep against our will."

Something dark passed over her face as she continued. "That is the way of Astaroth, the book's creator. As one of the first Nephilim, he was not content to rule over men. He sought dominion over us as well. His hunger for power drove him to the darkest arts, and in time, he forged spells capable of bringing even the oldest of our kind to their knees. The Sleep was one of them. Banishment was another. But his magic was designed to subjugate us, not mortals like you."

"Yet I'm banished here too," I said.

"Only because you clung to us in the moment of our banishment," Orionde replied. "But you are not bound here as we are. Which means, Maugis," she held my gaze, "you have the power to set us free."

I ran a hand through my hair, my mind racing. If I had the power to free them, did I even want to? Angelica had risked everything to cast them down here. She had been willing to tear everything down, all for the truth that had been stolen from her. How could I help Orionde and Una without knowing whether they truly deserved saving?

"First, I want some answers," I said, my voice sharp. "Why did you lie to Angelica about her parents? And why did you banish Morgain, one of your own?"

Orionde closed her eyes briefly and sighed.

"Morgain was not among those of us who first left Avalon for Rosefleur. Instead, she stayed in Avalon until about twenty-seven years ago. Unbeknownst to us, she took a mortal lover, a Frankish man named Accolon. That itself was forbidden among our kind, but then something happened that was unheard of. Morgain became with child."

I stiffened. That was the one thing Angelica had been desperate to know. The thing Orionde had stolen from her.

"Before then, we did not believe one of our kind could conceive by a mortal's seed. While it's true that the males among us, who mated with human women, fathered an entire race of Nephilim, it had never happened the other way around."

"Until Angelica," I murmured.

"Yes." Orionde hesitated. "Morgain must have used her powers to hide her pregnancy. She was always quite adept at casting glamours, and we did not know she had had the child. That was, until Una happened upon Morgain and Accolon in a glade in the forest, when she saw the infant swaddled in a blanket, lying in a crib woven from branches."

"Morgain swore me to secrecy," Una admitted, her voice quiet. "But when I overcame my shock, I knew I had to tell Orionde."

"That's why Angelica called you the betrayer."

Una nodded, eyes downcast, unable to meet my gaze.

"What happened on the day Accolon died?" I asked.

Orionde's jaw tightened, but she did not look away. 'We waited until she and Accolon returned to the glade," she said. "I demanded that she and the child return to Rosefleur. But Accolon flew into a rage. He drew his sword and attacked. I parried his blows with my own blade, but he lunged and made a wild strike. My sword pierced his heart before I could bring it down."

She exhaled, and for the first time, her voice wavered.

"Even with our healing arts, there was no saving him. And watching him die ..." She looked away for a moment. "I do not know if I can blame Morgain for what she did next."

"What did she do?"

"She set the glade afire. The very earth beneath her cracked. She swore Rosefleur would burn, that we would all pay. It took six of my sisters, including Una, to restrain her. But even by the next day, her anger had not faded. It was as if Accolon's death had broken something in her mind. She would not stop. She would have destroyed us all."

Orionde's eyes locked onto mine. "We had no choice, Maugis. We did what was necessary."

"You banished her."

"We thought it was the only way to prevent her vengeance. Yet now, I fear she may have succeeded."

I swallowed hard. Without my help, Angelica would have triggered the ward in the library and alerted Orionde before we could find the *Book of Shadows*. Then, none of this would have happened. And yet, would that have been better? If Angelica had never learned the truth, would she have been spared from all of this? Or would she have spent her life yearning for something she could never name?

Despite my shame, my thoughts returned to her. "So you raised Angelica at Rosefleur and never told her about her mother and father?"

"Did we have a choice?" Orionde asked, frustration edging her voice. "We did not know what she was or what she might become. And we still don't. She has none of the characteristics of the Nephilim, their great height and physical strength. But might she share their longevity? A Nephilim of Gog can live seven hundred years. Will Angelica, too? She's only half-mortal, and it's her divine half that concerned us. So, we decided we had to observe her until we learned what she was. That is why I never taught her the secrets I'd taught you. I do not know what she might do with that knowledge."

"But you taught her the power."

"We knew she would learn how to use it one way or another," Orionde admitted. "For as Morgain's child, it flowed through her veins. We thought it better to teach her our way instead of having her develop it on her own, uncontrolled and reckless. That might have made her more dangerous than she is now. Or at least she was."

I narrowed my gaze. "What do you mean?"

"I fear Morgain may be poisoning her mind," Orionde explained, "but far worse is the influence of the *Book of Shadows*. That book does not merely contain knowledge. It corrupts. Astaroth's will lingers in every page, whispering to the reader, shaping their thoughts before they even realize it. If he has reached Angelica, it might be too late to save her."

A sharp pain twisted in my chest.

Without me, she never would have found that book.

My head slumped into my palms. A breath hitched in my throat, and I choked back a sob.

Forcing myself to breathe, I lifted my chin.

"We have to save her."

Orionde didn't answer at first. Her gaze flickered downward for a moment before she met my eyes again.

"Then we best get moving," she said. "For we have much work to do."

PART THREE
LABYRINTH

CHAPTER 23

THE CAPTIVE

Maugis hung there, wrists and ankles bound in the silky web, his skull pounding with every shallow breath. His lips were cracked, his throat parched, his body drained. He wanted to close his eyes, to feel cool water on his tongue, to be done with this tale.

Or die, if death was what awaited him.

The effects of her potion were fading. He could feel it. The weight in his mind was lifting, the haze thinning. But not enough, not yet. The compulsion still gripped him, held fast like the web around his limbs. He could not resist her commands.

"Tell me how you escaped the Riverlands." Nimue sat perched on her stool, amusement glinting in her eyes, as if she were watching a mummers' show.

Maugis croaked out a sigh. "It took three days, and it almost killed me. There was no food in that hellish place, and while there was water in the rivers, none of it was safe to drink. I spent the first day scouring through the caves in the basalt cliffs. We found bones, the remains of four-legged beasts with torn hides stiff as leather. There were manlike skeletons, too, in those caves."

He hesitated, the memory stabbing like needles. The skeletons had been wrong. Too long in the limbs, their skulls oddly shaped, their fingers ending in claws.

"I doubt they were human," Maugis said. "Orionde told me little about them. All she had said was they, too, had been banished. And here, they had died."

Maugis exhaled sharply and shook his head, forcing the image away.

"Orionde and Una used the power to bind the bones and leathery hide into a small boat. They called it a currach. From more bones, they made oars, a finishing touch to our boat of the dead. Then they quelled the flames of Phlegethon long enough for us to paddle across it. The heat was unbearable. My skin felt as if it might peel from my bones. But I survived.

"From there, we trekked for more than a day across ash-gray plains beneath the oppressive gloom of the sky, dragging our currach behind us. By the third day, hunger was consuming me, and my throat was bone dry. I was becoming so weak that Una had to support me at times. Each step felt heavier than the last. I don't even remember reaching the Lethe. Only that I was walking, and the next, I was on my knees, barely able to keep my eyes open. We paddled until we found the cave that entered into the lake. But the cave's mouth was filled with mists, and only my soul light could breach the barrier."

Maugis clenched his jaw, remembering the sheer effort it had taken.

"My crystal had been set into my ring, so I had it on me. But summoning my soul light took almost more strength than I had left. I fell unconscious. Orionde and Una must have rowed our currach through the breach in the mists. When I woke, I was on the lakeshore, back where Angelica had banished us."

He paused, then his voice dropped to a whisper. "But she and Morgain were gone."

Nimue's brow knit into a frown. "Is that all?"

Maugis exhaled a ragged breath. "No."

He forced air into his lungs, gathering what strength he could. "We saw the smoke still rising from Rosefleur's windows. As Orionde's sisters lay trapped in the Sleep, Angelica and Morgain set fire to the library. Thousands of years of knowledge turned to ashes. Una was inconsolable when she gazed upon the damage. The shelves were steaming and burnt out, their contents gone. Black ash dusted the walls and floated through the air like motes of dust."

Nimue tilted her head slightly. "Just the library?"

Maugis tried to nod, but his head was too heavy. "Orionde built that library with her own hands. It was her pride, her devotion, the heart of all she sought to preserve. I suppose that Angelica and Morgain knew that if they wished to wound her, this was the best way to do it."

A ghost of a smile formed on Nimue's lips as if she took pleasure in Orionde's pain. She sipped from her wine flute, then flicked a long strand of her silver hair over her shoulder.

"Tell me what happened to Morgain and Angelica."

Maugis squeezed his eyes shut. The memory cut through him like a jagged knife.

"No," he growled. "I'm done."

Nimue's eyes flared, the glimmer of amusement vanishing in an instant. "You are done when I say you're done!"

Her lips curled into a scowl. "I see my elixer is wearing off. But I have more where that came from." She rose from her stool, her gaze never leaving him. "Watch over him, my pets, until I return."

As she strode toward an iron-bound door set into the trunk of the titanic stone-gray tree, a clicking sound filled Maugis' ears. A glossy white spider scuttled up his chest, its eight black eyes fixed on his face. It hissed, the sharp tips of its mandibles glistening with venom. Then, with deliberate slowness, it raised one of its forelegs and tapped him sharply between the eyes.

Maugis winced, then turned his head away. As he steadied his breath, he could feel his will clawing its way back from the darkness, inch by inch.

His thoughts drifted to his friends. Roland, Turpin, Bradamante.

Had she caught them, too? Or has she killed them?

A shudder ran through him, but he forced the thought aside.

It cannot end like this ...

CHAPTER 24

THE HOUNDS
OF ANNWN

Roland could only imagine how long they had been lost in this labyrinth of tunnels.

Hours? A day?

The tunnels all looked the same now: rough stone walls, twisted passageways, eerie patches of phosphorescent lichen casting a sickly light. They had trudged through one after another, reaching fork after fork, choosing at random and hoping and praying that one would lead them back to the White Spring, or to the shore of the strange, glowing lake, if they had any hope of saving Maugis, if he was even alive.

Roland's heart sank as his eyes landed on the corpse of the hound.

A curse slipped from his lips.

Turpin let out a long sigh. "We've been going in circles."

Roland stood there, numb, staring at the corpse. The creature was as large as a wolfhound, with hairless, pale skin stretched tight over sinewy limbs. Its pointed ears were pulled back from its head, and a black tongue lolled out of its long mouth, filled with jagged teeth. A black eye, dull and lifeless, fixed on the ceiling.

His hand fell to his side, beneath his ribs, where the beast's teeth had ripped through his chainmail, through his leather gambeson, and into his flesh. The wound still ached, and the blood, though mostly dry and crusted, remained wet and sticky in places. Still, it was better than the huge gash the other beast rent into Turpin's shoulder. Those two hounds—if they could even be called hounds—had nearly killed them. And there was at least one, if not two of the beasts, still roaming about in this maddening maze of tunnels.

Roland's muscles still ached from the battle. It had happened so fast that, before he knew it, they'd lost sight of Bradamante.

Earlier that night, when the Fae woman attacked Maugis, Turpin had to pull Roland back.

"We have to flee," the archbishop had growled. "We can't help him dead."

The events that followed remained seared in Roland's mind. First, gastly howls filled the cavern as the pale creatures by the woman's feet sprang to life.

Then, Bradamante flew past them, and in a heartbeat, they were charging after her, back into the tunnels. As soon as they entered the one from which they arrived, the mists came.

It rose from nowhere, wet and silvery, swallowing everything beyond an arm's length.

"Roland!" he heard Bradamante cry, but her voice was not near.

Next came the howls and barks, fierce and growing louder by the second.

Turpin pulled him toward the opening of another

tunnel. Over his shoulder, Roland glimpsed the first flash of pale flesh through the misty veil.

"Shields!" Roland yelled as the thought sprang to his mind. "We form a wall here."

Turpin nodded as he pulled his shield off his back. Roland had barely worked his left arm through the straps and clutched the grip when the beasts struck.

Two of the hounds barreled into the shields, teeth tearing into the leather covering, claws raking at the willow boards. The force of their charge caused both men to stagger back, but they held their shields firm. Roland reached for his dirk and stabbed through the narrow gap between their shields. He felt the blade punch through flesh as one of the hounds let out a painful yowl. The hounds retreated a step, and through the gap in the shields, Roland saw spittle flying from their snapping jaws.

Their eyes burned like embers, gleaming with an intelligence that sent a shiver through Roland's bones.

The hounds charged again, but this time, they leaped. Roland raised his shield, but the beast landed on it with its full weight, driving Roland back into the passageway. Its curved claws gripped the shield's iron rim, trying to pull it down. For an instant, the beast succeeded. Jagged teeth scraped against the cheek plate of Roland's helmet, and hot spit splattered into his eyes. Its breath stunk of carrion rot.

The beast's hind paws clawed into Roland's unprotected thighs, shredding his woolen breeches and slicing into flesh.

Roland roared in pain as he slammed his shield and the beast into the rock wall as hard as he could. The hound slid off his shield but landed on all four of its massive paws, its eyes burning with feral rage. It lunged so fast that Roland could not raise his shield, but his dirk was there, and he plunged it into the beast's neck. Its jaws bit into Roland's side, chain links snapping and scattering through the air. It tore through the leather gambeson beneath his mail, sinking teeth into flesh and muscle.

Ignoring the pain, he ripped his dirk free and thrust it again into the neck, forcing the blade upward into the beast's skull. The hound let out a choking yelp. Its jaws went slack as Roland twisted the blade, watching the light dim from its eyes.

As he pushed the hound's dead weight off him, he heard Turpin cry out. His shield lay on the ground, and he was wrestling the hound, whose jaws clamped onto his shoulder. Blood pooled through his mail coat. Muscles bunched beneath his sleeves as Turpin grabbed the beast by its ribs. He tore it off, strands of bloody flesh still clinging to its jaws, and flung it to the ground.

Roland reached for Durendal's hilt and tore it from its scabbard. But before he could even ready his sword, the hound twisted and sprang to its feet. Its ember-like eyes flared, then narrowed, as it shrank back a step.

Roland could barely believe what he was seeing.

When Turpin threw the beast off, his silver cross, which he usually wore tucked beneath his mail, came free and swung at his chest. The hound turned its head as if it could not even look at the holy symbol.

Turpin realized it, too. He pulled the cross from its chain and thrust it toward the hound. With a whimper, the beast shrank back, then turned and vanished into the mist.

They had not seen the hounds since, nor had they found any sign of the third beast or of Bradamante. She must have taken a different passage deeper into the labyrinth. He worried for his cousin but knew she was strong and resourceful. He tried not to think about a worse outcome. That would not help any of them right now.

He stared down at the corpse of the hound he had killed however long ago. "What the hell do we do now?" he asked Turpin, frustrated.

Turpin gripped the silver cross in his left hand. "First thing we do is keep our faith. Bradamante's still out there somewhere, and Maugis may be alive, too."

Roland nodded, though when he last saw Maugis, the man hadn't looked in any condition to help them. Turpin was being too optimistic, but he listened, still.

"Both of them are clever," Turpin went on, "and perhaps one of them will find us. But until then, we have to fend for ourselves. We know we're in a labyrinth, and happening upon this poor beast shows we're doing a poor job of navigating through it. So, I suggest we remember what mythology taught us. We're not the first souls to enter a labyrinth, and the Greek hero Theseus came up with a fine way to find his way through one."

Roland thought for a moment. He was never one to mind his lessons on mythology, philosophy, and whatever else those ancient Greeks were fond of.

"How did he do it?" Roland asked.

"He used a ball of yarn to mark his path." Turpin ran a hand through his beard. "We lack one of those, so we'll have to improvise. But I have some ideas."

"I'll try anything at this point," Roland sighed. "So let's get on with it."

CHAPTER 25

BRADAMANTE VALOROSA

Bradamante knew she could not turn back. She also knew she had to keep right in this maze of passageways, because that's where the water had come from.

She had discovered that shortly after she lost Roland and Turpin in the sudden mist and ducked down the nearest tunnel. With the hound's snarls echoing behind her, she had raced through the twisting tunnels, her heart hammering. That is when she saw it: a fissure in the rock wall where water, pale and glowing like moonlight, gushed into a yard-wide stream that disappeared through another crack in the far wall. Bradamante leapt across the stream, only to hear the hound skid to a halt. Its ferocious barking died to a whimper in the face of the running water.

It won't cross it, she realized.

She had no idea why. Any other type of hound would have charged straight through the water and overtaken her. But this strange beast, whose hairless hide reflected the same paleness as the water, now stood at the edge of the stream, pacing like a guard dog, a low growl rumbling from its long snout.

Whatever the hound's motives were, one thing was certain: the water was coming from the lake. Which meant the rock wall to her right must be close to the shore. With luck, this tunnel would lead her there. So, every time her path had forked, she had chosen the one to the right.

As much as she wanted to escape these gloomy tunnels, she worried about Roland and Turpin. The other two hounds were likely still hunting them, and though both were seasoned warriors, fighting beasts was nothing like fighting men. She had known wolves, boars, and even stags, to bring down even the most capable warriors. Yet it was her thoughts of Maugis that concerned her the most. His painful cry still echoed in her mind. The thought of that witch torturing him—or worse, killing him—set Bradamante's blood aflame. If she found that witch again, she would run her blade through the woman's heart.

Bradamante trudged through the twisting tunnels for an hour perhaps, maybe more. It was hard to keep track of time in these dim passageways, with only patches of the strange lichen giving off any light. The tunnel forked two more times, and each time, she stayed to the right. She pressed her palm against the rock wall. It was cold.

And damp.

This has to work, she told herself.

More time passed. Eventually, the lichen's faint light gave way to a pale glow. Her spirits rose.

A way out!

She quickened her pace toward the light.

A few steps later, her heart sank. Instead of exiting at the lake's shore, the tunnel opened into a roughly round chamber with a curved, dome-like ceiling. Pale light streamed in through narrow crevices, cut like crude windows into the rock.

She stepped into the chamber. The light glinted off a series of silvery drawings on the ceiling, fifteen feet above, but everything else it touched was ash and char. Thick soot blackened the walls and the chamber's only fixture, a flat stone table near the left wall, shaped like an altar. The unburnt patches of floor were covered in heaps of dark gray ash. One pile near her boot looked like the remnant of a book. She touched it with the tip of her sword, and it crumbled into a shapeless mound of ashes. Similar remnants were scattered around the room, and Bradamante wondered if a small library had been set aflame. Whatever had happened here, it was long ago. There was not a trace of smoke left in the air. Only the damp, earthy scent of the Lethe drifting in through the narrow crevices.

She strode toward the crevice-like windows, noting that the tunnel continued on into darkness at the far end of the chamber. Though barely wider than her arm, the crevices were a yard long and roughly shaped, as if some gigantic three-taloned beast had torn a deep wound in the side of the rock wall. Peering through the crevices, she looked out at the glowing lake. On an island at the lake's center stood the colossal oak tree, its highest branches vanishing into Avalon's gloom. She squinted, catching movement in the sprawling branches halfway up the massive trunk.

Her breath caught, and her hand flew to her mouth.

Between the branches stretched a vast, spider-like web, and at its center hung a man, limbs splayed like a victim on a torturer's rack. She had no doubt who it was.

Maugis.

Her chest tightened as she imagined his fear, as he faced whatever horror had spun such a web. The thought of losing him pressed deeper into her chest. She had watched men die before, on the battlefield, more times than she could count. Men she admired and respected, good men. But Maugis ... she could not lose him. Not now. And not at the hands of this witch.

Fury rose hot in her veins. If she could kill the witch, perhaps she could still save him. But she was trapped in this maze, with no way to reach the island. Bradamante exhaled slowly, leaning against the cold rock wall.

How will I get out of here?

She tipped her head up as if hoping for an answer from above. That was when she noticed the markings again on the domed ceiling. They shone silver, penetrating the soot and covering the open spaces like stars filling a night sky. But they were bound by lines into shapes. Familiar ones, too.

Those are astrological constellations, she realized.

She followed the constellations across the dome until they disappeared into the far wall. But there was something else etched on that wall. She started across the room, then paused when her boot stepped on something hard. She reached down and found the obstruction buried within a pile of ash. A crystal, about the size of a hazelnut. She wiped soot and ash from its surface with her thumb. It appeared cloudy, finely cut, and faintly translucent, like the one set into Maugis' ring. The one he used to summon his soul light.

She tucked the crystal into a belt pouch and continued toward the wall. It was covered in thick soot, but she swore there was writing beneath. Using the sleeve of her already weather-stained tunic, she began wiping the grime away. Sure enough, there were words carved into the stone. Most were in some foreign tongue. Yet scattered among them were names she recognized:

Arthur … Camelot … Morgain …

She scrubbed at the soot, uncovering more names:

Lancelot … Guinevere … Mordred …

By the time she had revealed the final carvings, her sleeves were black. There were two more names and two more words. But unlike the rest, these words were written in Latin.

Camlann … Death … Lethe … Tomb …

The last word sparked a memory of something Father Meical had said about the old prophet, Merlin. The Lady of the Lake kept him imprisoned, like a marble ornament decorating a mausoleum.

Like a tomb.

Her jaw dropped as the thought struck. She reached back into her belt pouch and pulled out the crystal.

"Could this have belonged to Merlin?" she muttered.

Her mind began to race. If it was Merlin's crystal, could he still be out there somewhere, imprisoned beneath the Fae woman's curse?

There was only one way to find out.

CHAPTER 26

MERLIN'S TOMB

Bradamante entered the tunnel on the other side of the soot-stained chamber. She moved cautiously beneath the dim, eerie glow of violet and lime-green lichen splattered across the rock walls. When the passageway forked, she stayed to the right, placing a palm on the cold stone wall, confident that the Lethe was on the other side.

After a series of winding turns, the lichen's light faded, giving way to a pale moonlight glow. Hope swelled in her chest. The tunnel opened into the vast cavern of the lake. But instead of the sandy gray shore, a cluster of tiny islands dotted the lake, forming a landscape like a peat bog. Tall reeds sprang from the dark earth, though they appeared as petrified as the titanic tree looming a quarter mile away. High in its branches, the vast web shimmered faintly, though its ensnared victim was nothing more than a distant speck.

There was no lakeshore leading back to the tree. Instead, the glowing waters of the Lethe lapped against the cavern walls. She peered across the cluster of small islands, their jagged crescent shape meandering halfway across the lake. On the farthest island, something jutted up from the earth. Roughly rectangular, it reminded her of a burial mound.

Or a tomb.

The nearest island, no larger than an overturned fishing boat, lay just five feet from the rocky shore where the tunnel opened. A narrow band of glowing water separated the two. She recalled what Maugis had told her about the waters of the Lethe, and a shiver ran down her skin.

Its name means "oblivion" … if you were to drink of its waters, you would forget who you ever were …

She steeled her nerves and took a deep breath. *If I make it across, the water won't matter.*

She started forward and leapt toward the island, her boots crunching against the gray gravel on its surface. Reaching out, she brushed her fingers over one of the petrified reeds. Its tip was as sharp as a spear's blade. Hundreds more sprang from the tiny islands, and she realized how dangerous this game of leapfrog would be. Not only did she have to stay out of the water, but she also had to avoid skewering herself on the reeds.

With care, she hopped to the next island, only two feet away. But the isle after that was nearly four times as far, and the glowing expanse of water stretched before her like a deadly chasm. She sprinted forward, weaving between the sharp reeds, then clenched her fists and leaped as far as she could. She landed hard, arms flailing as she fought to steady herself to avoid toppling onto a cluster of spear-like reeds.

Catching her breath, she counted five more islands

before the one with the tomb-like mound. The next two were fairly close. She traversed them with two deft hops, then muttered a curse.

The next island was twice as large as any before it, only six feet away. But it was covered with reeds, like a giant gray sea urchin washed ashore. She searched for a safe landing and spotted a narrow patch of ground amid the jutting spikes. With a short run, she vaulted over the watery gap but stumbled on impact. She threw out her hands to shield herself from the reeds and winced as they sliced into her palms. She barely caught herself before a shorter reed speared her through the chest. Thin red lines streaked across both hands.

"Dammit," she cursed under her breath.

She wiped her bleeding palms on her breeches and wove her way through the clusters of reeds. Ahead, she spotted a mound, larger than a round shield. At first, it seemed like a pile of pale gray rocks. Until she noticed the skull. The rest were bones.

And then, the bones moved.

Bradamante felt a surge of fear.

The skeletal horror rose to its feet, draped in the rusted remnants of ringmail, looming above her. It resembled the undead they had fought in the graveyard at Saint Julien's, but while those creatures had nothing but shadows in their hollow eye sockets, this one's skull burned with a pair of fiery orbs. A hiss rasped from its open mouth as it spread its arms, its fingers splayed like claws.

She drew her sword, but the undead warrior struck first. Claws tore through the mail on her left shoulder, shredding rings, leather, and flesh beneath. She cried out as a biting cold flooded the wound. Gritting her teeth, she swung hard, striking its arm, but her sword clattered off bone as unyielding as stone. It raked at her again with a flurry of strikes, and she barely kept up, parrying strike after strike. She matched its speed, but it was driving her back toward the deadly reeds.

With a backhand strike, she slammed the flat of her blade into the creature's skull. It shook its head, hardly flinching. She struck again, but this time, the creature caught her sword's blade in its hands. While she could match its speed, she could not match its strength. She yanked with all her might, but the blade wouldn't budge. It tightened its grip. An eerie frost spread up and down the blade. Then, with a crack, it shattered like glass.

She gasped, dropping the freezing remains of her sword; its hilt and shattered steel clattered to the ground.

The creature's free hand lashed out, seizing Bradamante by the neck. Icy claws dug into her skin. With inhuman strength, it shoved her backward. She felt the reed punch through the back of her already wounded shoulder. The creature forced her down the reed's stalk, impaling her. Agony exploded through her chest, driving the air from her lungs, as the skeleton's claws tightened around her throat.

She could not breathe.

Her right hand scrabbled across the ground, searching for anything to fight with. Her fingers brushed against something: cold, jagged metal. A remnant of her sword. She closed her grip around the broken blade, the edge biting into her skin. With the last of her strength, she slammed the remains of her blade into the creature's skull. A curl of smoke hissed from the bone, and the apparition let out a rasping wail. Its fingers released her neck.

Where she had struck, a blackened crucifix burned into its forehead. She realized she was gripping the broken blade just beneath the guard, the ruined hilt forming the shape of a cross.

She smashed the makeshift cross into the creature's skull once more. Its ember-like eyes flared, then hissed into smoke. The light vanished from its hollow sockets. The skull teetered, then tumbled free, before the foul thing collapsed into a pile of bones.

She struggled to catch her breath, her shoulder pulsing with pain, blood spilling from where the reed had impaled her. She seized the stalk and wrenched it as hard as she could. The reed snapped with a sharp crack. She pulled it free from the wound, but blood pulsed from the gash. She clamped a hand over it, but the blood seeped through her fingers.

A cold dread filled her veins.

Gritting her teeth, she pushed herself to her feet. The next island was not far. Just a yard-long leap. She made the jump but landed hard, her wound throbbing on impact. Her mail coat, from shoulder to waist, was stained red. She shambled toward the next island. Just another yard. She leaped, barely catching herself on the shore. Her left arm hung limp, numb, and useless.

She gazed upon the final island, where the burial mound rose two feet above the tips of the spear-like reeds. A figure lay motionless on the mound's flat surface, just as Brother Meical had told them.

Like a marble ornament decorating a mausoleum.

"Merlin," she whispered.

The island was just six feet away. Though her limbs felt leaden, she ran and leaped. Her boot struck earth. She staggered, barely catching herself on the burial mound. Pain lanced through her shoulder as she pushed herself upright.

The man lying on the mound wore gray robes that

matched the pallor of his skin. He was tall but thin and older than she had imagined. Perhaps he had been handsome in life, with sharp cheekbones and a neatly cropped silver beard. Now, he lay utterly still, as if asleep. Not an inch of him had decayed.

She reached out, touching his clasped hands. His skin was as cold as a corpse.

This is my last chance, she thought.

She plucked the crystal from her belt pouch and wedged it beneath his hands while Brother Meical's words echoed in her mind.

A kiss, born of true love, might yet break the bindings that hold him.

Bending down, she pressed her lips against his. It felt like kissing cold stone. She drew back and sighed.

Nothing happened.

"I'm not his true love," she muttered. Sebile had been, and she had died long ago. There was no one left to wake him. But what else had Brother Meical said?

Love, once lost, may rise again, reflected in another's eyes …

"Damn these riddles!"

She pressed a trembling hand to her forehead, feeling faint. Out of the corner of her eye, she caught the distant image of the tree rising from the glowing lake, the web between its branches glistening in the water's light.

"Maugis."

She knew then what her heart felt, but her mind refused to accept.

Maugis.

Gazing down at Merlin, she imagined he was Maugis. *Her Maugis.*

She bent down, closed her eyes, and kissed his lips, long and tender, imagining for a moment that he returned her kiss.

When she opened her eyes, it was not Maugis who lay there, but Merlin. His face was a cold, lifeless mask.

She clutched at her wound, still pulsing with blood. Her world began to waver.

So this is how it ends, she thought.

Then Merlin's eyelids began to flutter.

The story concludes in **MERLIN REBORN.**

HISTORICAL NOTE

My goal in this prequel series was to reimagine some of the classic stories about the Paladins of Charlemagne and tie them to the broader narrative that unfolds in the main trilogy, comprised of *Enoch's Device, The Key to the Abyss,* and *The Cauldron of God.* Like all the books in my *Dragon-Myth Cycle* series, there are elements rooted in history, though the prequel is much more fantasy-centered. That's because these stories are based on the fantasy-heavy legends surrounding the paladins, which derive from late medieval French poems known as *chansons de geste* or "songs of deeds."

The only real history in *The Sorceress of Avalon* appears at the beginning of Angelica's Tale, where Maugis recounts Charlemagne's campaign to suppress Hunald's rebellion in Aquitaine in 769. This occurred early in Charlemagne's reign, a year after his father, Pepin the Short, died, leaving his growing kingdom divided between Charles (Charlemagne) and his brother, Carloman. This was three years before Charlemagne's first Saxon campaign in 772 and six years before the events in *Hela's*

Bane, when Charlemagne was commanding vast armies to expand his rule into what would be known as the Carolingian Empire.

Roland, the epic hero of *The Song of Roland*, was a real historical figure who served as the military governor of the Breton March and died at Roncevaux in 778. Turpin, the legendary warrior-bishop, is based on the historical Archbishop Tilpin of Reims, though his presence in Aquitaine at this time is uncertain. Maugis, Bradamante, and Angelica are characters from the *chansons de geste* with no historical counterparts. Everything we know about them comes from late medieval and Renaissance tales.

The *chansons de geste* were epic poems that focused on Charlemagne and his paladins. While they flourished in France, another literary movement was growing in Europe: Arthurian romance. This movement began with Geoffrey of Monmouth's *Historia Regum Britanniae* (circa 1136), which transformed King Arthur from a vague warlord into a legendary king and introduced magic-using characters like Merlin and Morgana le Fay. Chrétien de Troyes built upon Geoffrey's work in the twelfth century, adding courtly love and chivalry with stories such as *Lancelot, the Knight of the Cart* and *Perceval, the Story of the Grail*.

By the late Middle Ages, these two traditions began to mix, and characters like Merlin and Morgana began appearing in stories about the paladins of Charlemagne. The Italian Renaissance built upon these medieval legends, transforming them into fantastic adventures with magic swords and Merlin-like sorcerers. One of those was Maugis d'Aygremont, resurrected from the old *chansons de geste*.

The Sorceress of Avalon reimagines portions of several of these epic tales. In the Renaissance romance *Orlando Furioso* by Ludovico Ariosto, Bradamante visits Merlin's tomb, where she speaks with his ghost during a quest to reunite with her love, Ruggiero. This inspired Bradamante's journey in this novella, though I have substituted Maugis for Ruggiero for the sake of the story. Angelica is also a major character in *Orlando Furioso*. There, she is a princess of Cathay (China) and an enchantress, but as I explained in the historical note to *The Fae Dealings*, I completely reimagined her for this series. While Maugis' backstory is rooted in earlier *chansons de geste*, he, too, appears in the Renaissance stories of Angelica and Bradamante. But his role as Angelica's lover is my own creation.

Nimue, the Lady of the Lake, is not featured in the *chansons de geste* or the Renaissance romances, though she is a famous figure in Arthurian mythology and plays a significant role in my second novel, *The Key to the Abyss*. However, Morgana—or Morgain here—appears in several of the Renaissance narratives about the paladins of Charlemagne. In these tales, she's one of the Fae, a seductive enchantress who lures knights into her magical domain like the fairy queens of old. She is often associated with Oiger the Dane, one of Charlemagne's paladins and the fictional ancestor of Holger Horrikson from *The Key to the Abyss* and *The Cauldron of God*. I've reimagined Morgain's story, placing her in Maugis' tale and creating her secret connection to Angelica.

That leaves us with the *Book of Shadows*. There is a book with this name in the Wiccan tradition, but I've envisioned it as a medieval grimoire. I also drew upon H.P. Lovecraft's *Necronomicon* and even Marvel's *Darkhold* as inspiration for this tome of forbidden magic. As for its author, Astaroth is one of the few demons mentioned by name in the *Legends of Charlemagne*. And all the stories about this duke of hell involve Maugis d'Aygremont. So, there will be much more about these characters to come as the series reaches its thrilling conclusion in *Merlin Reborn*.

ABOUT THE AUTHOR

Joseph Finley writes historical fantasy that mixes medieval history, myth, and a dash of magic. He's a longtime fan of knights, old legends, classic fantasy paperbacks, and wandering through castles and cathedrals on his travels. Most evenings you'll find him with a glass of wine in hand, and most mornings he's back at it, surrounded by history books and chasing down the next story.

To receive a **<u>free short story</u>**, as well as updates on Joseph's next novel and special offers, join his Reader List by signing up **here** or at his website, below:

www.authorjosephfinley.com

Lastly, if you enjoyed this book, please consider leaving a review (even if it's only a line or two) at Amazon or Goodreads. Word-of-mouth is essential to an author's success, so your input is greatly appreciated!

facebook.com/AuthorJosephFinley

x.com/joseph_finley

instagram.com/josephfinley

www.ingramcontent.com/pod-product-compliance
Lightning Source LLC
Chambersburg PA
CBHW032251070726
47590CB00016B/2429